King Arthur's Socks
and Other Village Plays

Floyd Dell

Contents

KING ARTHUR'S SOCKS
AND OTHER VILLAGE PLAYS

BY

Floyd Dell

HUMAN NATURE

A VERY SHORT MORALITY PLAY

TO ARTHUR DAVISON FICKE

This is a much changed version of "A Five Minute Problem Play," originally given at the Liberal Club, New York City, in 1913.

Boundless blue space. Two celestial figures stand in front of it, talking. One of them carries a pointer, such as is used in class-room demonstrations at the blackboard. The other has a red-covered guidebook under his arm.

THE FIRST CELESTIAL FIGURE (*the one with the pointer*) Well, I think that is all. You've seen everything now.

THE SECOND CELESTIAL FIGURE (*the One With the guidebook*) It has all been very interesting, and I don't know how to thank you for the trouble you've taken.

THE FIRST CELESTIAL FIGURE. Don't mention it. That's my business, you know--to show young and curious Spirits what there is to see in the universe. And I must say that you've been an exceptionally patient pupil. I don't usually take as much time with youngsters as I have with you. But when I find someone as interested in the universe as you are,

I don't mind spending a few more eons on the job. We've been all around, this trip. I don't believe we've missed anything of any importance. But if there is anything else you can think of that you'd like to see--

THE SECOND CELESTIAL FIGURE. (*hesitantly*) Well, there is one place . . . It's only mentioned in a footnote in the guide-book, but for that very reason I thought perhaps--

THE FIRST CELESTIAL FIGURE. You have the right attitude. There's nothing too small or insignificant to know about. Do you remember the name of the place?

THE SECOND CELESTIAL FIGURE. No, but--(He turns the leaves of the guide-book.) Here it is. (He holds the book closer so as to read the fine print at the bottom of the page.) Earth, it's called.

THE FIRST CELESTIAL FIGURE. Ah, yes, there is such a place. . . .

THE SECOND CELESTIAL FIGURE. The guide-book doesn't give any information about it. Just mentions its name.

THE FIRST CELESTIAL FIGURE. Well, there isn't very much to say about it. After what you've seen, you wouldn't be impressed by its art or its architecture, . . . Still, it has one curious feature that perhaps you'd be interested in. It's--

He pauses.

THE SECOND CELESTIAL FIGURE. Yes?

THE FIRST CELESTIAL FIGURE. Perhaps I had better just show you, and let you make what you can of it.

THE SECOND CELESTIAL FIGURE. (*deferentially*) As you say.

THE FIRST CELESTIAL FIGURE. Here, then--look for yourself!

He raises the pointer, and boundless space rolls up like a curtain, disclosing a comfortable drawing-room. The two celestial figures stand aside and look. A man and woman are sitting on a sofa, kissing each other. From time to time, in intervals between the kisses, they speak.

THE MAN. No! No! I must not!

But he does.

THE WOMAN. No! No! We must not!

But they do.

THE MAN. We must not--

The second celestial figure turns to look inquiringly at the first, and boundless space falls like a blue curtain between them and the scene.

THE SECOND CELESTIAL FIGURE. It is strange. I've seen nothing like that anywhere in the universe. But why do you suppose--

THE FIRST CELESTIAL FIGURE. Oh, as to that, I really cannot say. It's what is called "Human nature."

THE SECOND CELESTIAL FIGURE. Oh!

They walk off thoughtfully.

THE CHASTE ADVENTURES OF JOSEPH

A COMEDY

"The Chaste Adventures of Joseph" was first produced at the Liberal Club, New York City, in 1914, with the following cast:

Madam Potiphar .... Louise Murphy
Asenath .... Marjorie Jones
Potiphar .... Berkeley Tobey
Joseph .... Floyd Dell
Slave .... Maurice Becker

A room in Potiphar's house. It is sparingly furnished with a table, two stools, and a couch, all in the simpler style of the early dynasties.... The table, which is set at an angle, is piled with papyri, and one papyrus is half-unrolled and held open by paper-weights where somebody has been reading it.... There is a small window in one wall, opening on the pomegranate garden. At the back, between two heavy pillars, is a doorway.... Two women are heard to pass, laughing and talking, through the corridor outside, and pause at the doorway. One of them looks in curiously.

THE LADY. Such a lovely house, Madam Potiphar!--But what is this quiet room? Your husband's study?

MADAM POTIPHAR. (*coming in*) Oh, this is nothing--merely the room of one of the slaves. Come, dear Cousin Asenath, and I will show you the garden. The pomegranates are just beginning to blossom.

ASENATH. The room of a slave? Indeed! He seems to be an educated person!

MADAM POTIPHAR. Educated? Oh, yes--he is a sort of book-keeper for Potiphar. At least, that is what he is supposed to be. But he is never on hand when he is wanted. If he were here, we might get him to show us through the vineyard.

ASENATH. Why not send for him? I would love to see the vineyard before your husband takes me out in the chariot.

MADAM POTIPHAR. (*ironically*) Send for Joseph? It would be useless. Joseph has affairs of his own on hand, always.

ASENATH. (*startled*) Joseph! Is that his name?

MADAM POTIPHAR. Yes--"Joseph." An ugly, foreign-sounding name, don't you think?

ASENATH. It is rather an odd name--but I've heard it before. It was the name of a youth who used to be one of my father's slaves in Heliopolis.

MADAM POTIPHAR. Heliopolis? I wonder--what was he like?

ASENATH. Oh, he was a pretty boy, with nice manners.

MADAM POTIPHAR. I thought for a moment it might be the same one. But this Joseph is an ill-favoured creature--and insolent. . . . What colour was his hair?

ASENATH. I really don't remember. It's been a year since he was there.... You have a *lovely* house, my dear. I'm *so* glad I came to see you!

MADAM POTIPHAR. (*also willing to change the subject*) It's nice to see you again, dear Asenath. We haven't seen each other since we were little girls. Do you remember how we played together in the date-orchard? And the long, long talks we had?

ASENATH. Don't let's be sentimental about our childhood!
MADAM POTIPHAR. Do you remember how we talked about being married?
(*Asenath goes to the little window*.) We hated all men, as I remember.

ASENATH. I was eight years old then. . . . Who is that handsome young man I see out there?

MADAM POTIPHAR. In the garden?

ASENATH. Yes.

Madam Potiphar comes to the window.

MADAM POTIPHAR. That--that is the slave we were speaking of. . . .

ASENATH. Joseph? . . . I wonder if it *is* the same one? . . .

MADAM POTIPHAR. Well--and what if it were?

ASENATH. He was really a very interesting young man. . . .

MADAM POTIPHAR. If you are so anxious to find out, why don't you go and talk to him?

ASENATH. (*coolly*) I think I shall.

She starts toward the door.

MADAM POTIPHAR. (*shocked*) Asenath! You, a daughter of the High Priest of Heliopolis--

ASENATH. As such, I am quite accustomed to doing as I please.

She goes out.

MADAM POTIPHAR. (*looking amusedly after her*) Silly little thing! (*She stands there thinking*.) There's no doubt of it! Joseph did come from Heliopolis last year. But what have I to be afraid of? (She sees a pair of sandals on the floor by the table. She picks one of them up, and kisses it passionately, whispering)--Joseph!

Enter Potiphar. Madam Potiphar puts the sandal behind her back.

POTIPHAR. (*a dull, dignified gentleman*) Oh, here's where you are! I was looking everywhere for you. But where's your cousin?

MADAM POTIPHAR. She will be back in a moment. I brought her here to show her the educated slave of whom you are so proud, at work. But he is away somewhere, as usual.

POTIPHAR. (*defensively*) He has other duties.

MADAM POTIPHAR. Oh, yes, no doubt!

POTIPHAR. What's the matter now?

MADAM POTIPHAR. Nothing new. You know what I think about this Joseph of
yours.

POTIPHAR. (*irritated*) Now, if you are going to bring that
subject up again--! Well, I tell you flatly, I won't do it.

MADAM POTIPHAR. You'd better take my advice!

POTIPHAR. It's the most unreasonable thing I ever heard of! For the
first time in my life I get an efficient secretary--and you want me to
get rid of him. It's ridiculous. What have you against Joseph, anyway?

MADAM POTIPHAR. I--I don't think he's honest.

POTIPHAR. Honest! Who expects the secretary of a government official to
be honest? I don't want an honest man in charge of my affairs--all I
want is a capable one. Besides, how would I know whether he is honest
or not? I can't bother to go over his accounts, and I couldn't
understand them if I did. Mathematics, my dear, is not an art that
high-class Egyptians excel in. It takes slaves and Hebrews for that.

MADAM POTIPHAR. Well, just because he is able to add up a row of
figures is no reason why he should be so high-handed with everybody.
One would think he was the master here, instead of a slave.

POTIPHAR. A private secretary, my dear, is different from an ordinary
slave. You mustn't expect him to behave like a doorkeeper. I remember
now, he complained that you kept wanting him to run errands for you.

MADAM POTIPHAR. Yes, and he refused--in the most insolent manner. He

is
a proud and scheming man, I tell you. I am sure he is plotting some
villainy against you.

POTIPHAR. (*wearily*) Yes, you have said that before.

MADAM POTIPHAR. I say it again. Joseph is a scoundrel.

POTIPHAR. You'll have to do more than say it, my dear. What proof have
you of his villainy?

MADAM POTIPHAR. I think you might trust to my womanly intuition.

POTIPHAR. Bah! Joseph is going to stay! Do you understand?

He pounds on the table for emphasis. Madam Potiphar takes advantage
of the occasion to drop the sandal unnoticed.

MADAM POTIPHAR. Well, you needn't create a domestic scene. Asenath
may
return at any moment.

POTIPHAR. (*gloomily*) I believe I'm to take her out in the chariot.

MADAM POTIPHAR. You don't begrudge my guest that much of your
attention, do you? You know I cannot bear to ride behind those wild
horses of yours. And she said she wanted to see the city.

POTIPHAR. Oh--I'll go. But I must see to my chariot. (He claps his
hands. A servant appears, and bows deeply.) Send Joseph here at once.

With another deep bow, the slave disappears. A pause.

MADAM POTIPHAR. Now you know what it is to have your slave off attending to some business of his own when you want him.

POTIPHAR. (*annoyed*) Where can he be?

Enter Joseph.

JOSEPH. (ignoring Madam Potiphar, and making a slight bow to Potiphar) Here I am, sir.

POTIPHAR. (*after a triumphant glance at his wife*) Have my chariot made ready for me, will you?

JOSEPH. It will give me great pleasure to do so, sir.

He bows slightly, and goes out.

MADAM POTIPHAR. Did you notice his insolence?

POTIPHAR. There you go again! He said he was glad to do it for me. What more do you want?

MADAM POTIPHAR. You are the stupidest man in Egypt.

POTIPHAR. Thank you, my dear.

Joseph returns.

POTIPHAR. Is the chariot ready so soon, Joseph?

JOSEPH. The chariot is quite ready.

POTIPHAR. Very well. (*A pause*) And are those accounts finished yet,

Joseph?

JOSEPH. The accounts are quite finished. And I would like to suggest, if I may--

He is interrupted by the re-entrance of Asenath.

ASENATH. What a lovely garden you have!

MADAM POTIPHAR. (*significantly*) Yes!

ASENATH. The pomegranate blossoms are so beautiful!

MADAM POTIPHAR. You could hardly tear yourself away, could you?

POTIPHAR. (*with a patient smile*) And are you ready for your chariot ride now?

ASENATH. Oh, yes! I am so eager to see the city! But I fear my hair needs a touch or two, first. . . .

MADAM POTIPHAR. It is so hard to keep one's hair in order when one walks in the garden. I will take you to my room, dear Asenath. (To Potiphar) We shall be ready presently.

POTIPHAR. The horses are waiting!

ASENATH. It won't take me but a moment!

MADAM POTIPHAR. Come, my dear. (*They go toward the door*.) I am so glad you liked our garden--

They go out.

POTIPHAR. (*turning to Joseph*) What were you going to say, Joseph?

JOSEPH. You asked me about my accounts. I was about to suggest that I show them to you tonight, when you return from your ride.

POTIPHAR. (*alarmed*) No! No! I don't want to see them. . . . I just want to know that everything is getting on well.

JOSEPH. Everything is getting along quite well.

POTIPHAR. Very good. I have complete confidence in you. . . . Joseph-- you have a mathematical mind; how long would you say it would take a woman to do her hair?

JOSEPH. Not less than half an hour, sir--especially if she has something to talk about with another woman while she is doing it.

POTIPHAR. (*surprised*) What should *they* have to talk about?

JOSEPH. Secrets.

POTIPHAR. Secrets?

JOSEPH. What things are women especially interested in, sir?

POTIPHAR. Dress, perhaps?

JOSEPH. Perhaps.

POTIPHAR. Housekeeping?

JOSEPH. I doubt it, sir.

POTIPHAR. Joseph, you perturb me. Besides food and dress, there is only one subject, so far as I am aware, of interest to women. I hope you do not imply--

JOSEPH. Far be it from me, sir, to indulge in implications, with respect to an honoured guest, in the household in which I am a slave.

POTIPHAR. Still--it is hard to tell, sometimes. Women are mysterious creatures. What do *you* think of them, Joseph?

JOSEPH. I try not to, sir.

POTIPHAR. You are a wise man. Yes, I suppose you have your difficulties, too. The morality of the slave-girls is not all it should be. But if you will believe me, the morality of our women, too--

JOSEPH. Ah, sir!

POTIPHAR. Yes, Joseph, it leaves something to be desired. If you knew the advances that have been made to me by certain great ladies--

JOSEPH. If you will permit me to say so, sir, you have my sympathy.

POTIPHAR. Joseph--women are the very devil, aren't they?

JOSEPH. They are a great trial, sir. One must learn the secret of dealing with them.

POTIPHAR. Do *you* know that secret?

JOSEPH. I do, sir.

POTIPHAR. I am inclined to believe that you really do. You are a remarkable man. But then, you have a naturally cold disposition. It must come easy to you.

JOSEPH. Not so easy as you may think, sir. Temperamentally, I am very susceptible to the charms of women.

POTIPHAR. Then you are more remarkable even than I thought. Come, what *is* your secret?

JOSEPH. It is not the sort of secret that one gives away for nothing, sir.

POTIPHAR. I am sorry to see you display such a mercenary disposition, Joseph. But I see that I must come to terms with you. How much will you take to teach me your secret?

JOSEPH. This time, sir, I will not be mercenary. I will make you a sporting proposition.

POTIPHAR. (*very much interested*) Good! What is it?

JOSEPH. I will toss up a coin, and let you call it. If you win, I will teach you the secret for nothing. And if you lose--

POTIPHAR. And if I lose, you keep your secret--

JOSEPH. Not merely that. If you lose, you will give me my freedom.

POTIPHAR. But I cannot get along without you, Joseph!

JOSEPH. I will continue to work for you on a salary basis.

POTIPHAR. Done! Where is your coin?

Joseph takes a small coin from his wallet, flips it in the air, and covers it with his hand when it falls on the table. He looks up at Potiphar.

POTIPHAR. Much depends on this. What shall I say?

JOSEPH. I know what you will say, sir.

POTIPHAR. Impossible! Tails.

Joseph uncovers the coin. Potiphar bends over it.

JOSEPH. (*without looking*) It is heads.

POTIPHAR. So it is! I lose--Joseph, you are a lucky man!

JOSEPH. Not at all, sir--a clever one. You see, I knew just how the coin would fall. I tossed it so that it would fall that way.

POTIPHAR. But--how did you know what I was going to say?

JOSEPH. I will explain to you. On one side of the coin is a representation of the present Pharaoh, who has denied you advancement because of his daughter's interest in you. In consequence, you dislike any reminder of him--even on a coin. But on the other side is a representation of the goddess Isis; she is your favourite goddess--and moreover, you yourself have been heard to remark that her face and figure resemble remarkably that of a certain great lady, whose name--is never mentioned when the story is told. Naturally I knew how you would call the coin.

POTIPHAR. (*trembling with rage*) How dare you say such things! Do you forget that I can have you beaten with rods?

JOSEPH. (*calmly*) Do you forget, sir, that I am no longer a slave? Free men are not beaten in Egypt.

POTIPHAR. Free?

JOSEPH. Unless Potiphar takes back his word. It is true that I have no witnesses to it.

POTIPHAR. (*with great dignity*) Witnesses are unnecessary. I had forgotten for the moment. Let this remind me. (He gives Joseph a ring.) You are a free man. And so--what I thought was an insolence is merely a pleasantry. But--you take a quick advantage of your freedom.

JOSEPH. I accept the rebuke.

POTIPHAR. And--free man or slave--Joseph, you know too much!

Potiphar walks out of the room. . . . Joseph seats himself at the table, and takes up a scroll of papyrus. He reads a moment, then claps his hands. A slave enters, stands before the table, and bows.

JOSEPH. (*consulting the papyrus*) Bear word to the overseer of the winepress that the grapes in the southeast section will be brought in for pressing tomorrow morning. . . . Bear word to the chief carpenter that a table and two couches, of the standard pattern, are wanted--at once. . . . Bear word to the chief pastry-cook that his request for another helper is denied.

Joseph makes a gesture of dismissal, and the slave, with a bow, goes out. Joseph rises, and walking around the table, holds up 'his hand to look at his ring.

JOSEPH. Freedom!

Madam Potiphar strolls in.

MADAM POTIPHAR. (*familiarly*) They have gone. . . .

Joseph picks up a scroll from the table.

MADAM POTIPHAR. (*sharply*) Joseph!

JOSEPH. (*respectfully*) Yes, madam.

MADAM POTIPHAR. I understood you to say a while ago that your work was
quite finished?

JOSEPH. Yes, madam.

MADAM POTIPHAR. Then you have plenty of time now....

JOSEPH. Yes, plenty of time for more work.

MADAM POTIPHAR. Well, you need not begin immediately. *I* want a little of your time just now.

JOSEPH. If it is an errand, I will call one of the slaves.

MADAM POTIPHAR. Do you mean--one of the other slaves?

JOSEPH. I, madam, am no longer a slave.

He holds up his hand, and looks at the ring.

MADAM POTIPHAR. (*incredulous*) How did this happen? Did you *buy* your freedom, perchance?

JOSEPH. No. Your husband gave it to me a moment ago.

MADAM POTIPHAR. Gave it to you? You mean that you swindled him out of
it in some way!

JOSEPH. As you please, madam.

MADAM POTIPHAR. Well, it is his own affair if he wishes to give away
such valuable property. Only--it is difficult to adjust oneself to a
change like that.

JOSEPH. Do not, I pray, let the change disturb you.

MADAM POTIPHAR. No, I insist. It is both a duty and a pleasure. Since
you are now a free man, Joseph, I propose that we treat each other as
equals and friends.

JOSEPH. That will be very considerate of us both.

MADAM POTIPHAR. Sir, you are insolent. No, no--I mean, my friend, you
are very rude.

JOSEPH. Thank you for making the distinction. And now, since we are to
treat each other as equals and friends, I beg you--(he takes some
small objects from his wallet and holds them out in his hand)--to
take these hairpins, which are the mementos of your various visits to
my room. As a slave, no suspicion, of course, could attach to me in
connection with a lady of your rank. But as equals and friends, we both
have our reputations to preserve.

MADAM POTIPHAR. (*taking them*) Thank you.(She restores them to her hair.) I lose them everywhere I go. They fall out every time I speak. They mean nothing whatever.

JOSEPH. It is unnecessary to explain that to me. I am perfectly aware of the fact.

MADAM POTIPHAR. You are perfectly aware of everything, aren't you, Joseph?

JOSEPH. Everything that it is to my interest to be aware of, madam.

MADAM POTIPHAR. No--there is one thing you don't know, and I am going to tell you.

JOSEPH. Proceed, madam.

He takes the coin from the table.

MADAM POTIPHAR. (coming close to him and looking boldly into his eyes) Can't you guess?

At this moment Joseph drops the coin from his hand, and it rolls away. Joseph starts, looks after it, and goes across the room to pick it up.

JOSEPH. One must take care of the small coins!

MADAM POTIPHAR. (*angrily*) Oh!

She flings off to the window, Joseph returns and seats himself on the little stool at the nearer end of the table, with a papyrus in front of him. He reads it in silence. Madam Potiphar comes and seats herself on the table, and looks down at him. He continues to study the papyrus. She leans over to see what he is doing, and then, as he pays no attention, she turns so that she is reclining prone along its length, facing him, her chin in her hands, one foot idly waving in the air.

MADAM POTIPHAR. (*gently*) Am I bothering you?

JOSEPH. Not at all.

MADAM POTIPHAR. I like to watch you work.

JOSEPH. I don't mind.

MADAM POTIPHAR. You are very interesting to look at, do you know?

JOSEPH. (*absently*) Yes, I know.

MADAM POTIPHAR. Little egotist!

JOSEPH. (*unperturbed*) Yes.

He rises and seats himself at the side of the table. Propping his papyrus against the reclining body of Madam Potiphar, he takes a new sheet of papyrus, and commences to copy a passage.

MADAM POTIPHAR. (*wriggling about to look at him*) What are you copying?

JOSEPH. Be careful. Don't jiggle my manuscript, please!

MADAM POTIPHAR. I asked, what are you copying?

JOSEPH. I am copying some inaccurate information about the climate of Egypt, with reference to the yearly crop-yield. . . . I wonder if there is any one in Egypt who has exact information on that subject? . . .

MADAM POTIPHAR. The yearly crop-yield! What do you care about the yearly crop-yield?

JOSEPH. Never mind. You wouldn't understand if I told you.

MADAM POTIPHAR. You are quite right. Besides, I didn't come here to talk about crops.

JOSEPH. (*writing*) No. You came here to talk about me.

MADAM POTIPHAR. I came here to talk about my cousin Asenath. You knew
she was coming--why didn't you tell me you had been in service in her father's household in Heliopolis?

JOSEPH. (*writing*) It wasn't necessary for me to tell you. I knew she would.

MADAM POTIPHAR. No doubt you think we sat there all the time she was combing her hair, and talked about you!

JOSEPH. (*writing*) Precisely.

MADAM POTIPHAR. I suppose you know she is crazy about you!

JOSEPH. (***still writing***) Is she?

MADAM POTIPHAR. She doesn't put it just that way. She says she takes an interest in your future.

JOSEPH. (*continuing to work*) She doesn't take half as much interest
in it as I do.

MADAM POTIPHAR. She told me your romantic story: how you had been
sold
by your brothers into slavery because you wore a coat of many colours.
Joseph, did you wear a coat of many colours? That seems a curious thing
for any one to be angry about.

JOSEPH. (*not ceasing to copy the manuscript*) I wore it only
figuratively--I am wearing it now. And it *always* makes *you* angry.

MADAM POTIPHAR. You mean the cloak of your insolence?

JOSEPH. I mean the cloak of my pride.

MADAM POTIPHAR. I can sympathize with your brothers. . . . Are you in
love with her, Joseph?

JOSEPH. I am not.

He has finished--he rolls up the papyrus.

MADAM POTIPHAR. No--so I told her.

JOSEPH. But she didn't believe you.
MADAM POTIPHAR. You seem to know our conversation pretty well.

JOSEPH. I can imagine it.

MADAM POTIPHAR. Well, go ahead and imagine it. What did we say?

JOSEPH. You both lied to each other.

MADAM POTIPHAR. About what?

JOSEPH. About me.
MADAM POTIPHAR. (*sitting up*) Your conceit is insufferable!

JOSEPH. (*rising politely*) I hope so.

MADAM POTIPHAR. Is that a dismissal?

JOSEPH. If you will be so kind.

MADAM POTIPHAR. You interest me more and more.

JOSEPH. I feared as much.

MADAM POTIPHAR. I detest you!

JOSEPH. It is one of the symptoms.

MADAM POTIPHAR. Young man, do you really know nothing about love?

JOSEPH. If I don't, it is not the fault of the women of Egypt.

MADAM POTIPHAR. You are a strange youth. It cannot be that you love this work you are doing....

JOSEPH. No, madam--I *hate* it.

MADAM POTIPHAR. Then where do you find your happiness? Tell me, Joseph--what is the happiest hour of the day for you?

JOSEPH. (*with complete sincerity*) It is that hour when I have finished the day's work, and can lie down upon my couch. It is the hour before sleep comes, when the room is filled with moonlight, and there is no sound except the crickets singing in the orchard, and the music of the toads in the pool. The wind of the night comes in, cool with dew. Then I am happy--for I can lie and make plans for my future.

MADAM POTIPHAR. (*softly*) And in that hour of moonlight and dew and the music of the crickets, and the ancient love-song of the toads in the pool, when all the earth abandons itself to love,--what would you say to a woman who stole in to you like a moonbeam, like a breath of the night-wind, like a strain of music?

JOSEPH. I would tell her--to go, as her presence would interfere with my plans.

MADAM POTIPHAR. I call the gods to witness. A truly virtuous young man!

JOSEPH. (*jumping down from the table, angrily*) Virtue! Virtue! Oh, you stupid Egyptians! As though I cared about Virtue!

MADAM POTIPHAR. Well, what in the name of all the gods is it that you care about?

JOSEPH. (*vehemently*) In the name of all the gods, madam, I care about time.

MADAM POTIPHAR. Time! But what can you do with time?

JOSEPH. What can I do *without* it?

MADAM POTIPHAR. But I do not understand!

JOSEPH. (*in a cold rage*) Of course you do not understand. You are a great lady--and a fool. I am a wise man--and but an hour ago a slave. I have more intellect than all the population of Egypt put together. Do you expect me to be content to remain as I am? I want power and riches--and I intend to achieve them. And I cannot achieve them if I allow women to waste my time.

MADAM POTIPHAR. (*deeply angered at last*) Very well, I go--taking your secret with me! (*She goes*.)

JOSEPH. (*furiously, to the empty room*) Virtue! My God!

He sits down at his desk and writes vexedly.

*   *   *   *   *

Night. The room is filled with moonlight. Joseph is asleep at his desk.... He suddenly springs up in agitation.

JOSEPH. Ah! . . . It was only a dream! But what a dream! I thought I saw at the door--(*he points*) a strange and terrible animal! (*There is a sound at the door, and he starts back in terror*.) *There it is now*!

The curtains part, and Asenath enters, candle in hand.

ASENATH. Ssh! It is I--Asenath! Don't be afraid!

Joseph recovers his self-possession, and confronts her sternly.

JOSEPH. You, too!

ASENATH. My dear?

JOSEPH. So you have come to afflict me with more romantic folly!

ASENATH. (*with concern*) What is the matter with you, Joseph?

JOSEPH. What is the matter with me? Nothing is the matter with me. Why do you ask?

ASENATH. I think you are not well. You are behaving queerly. You must have been working too hard. How are your nerves?

She approaches him solicitously.

JOSEPH. (*retreating around the table*) Leave me alone, I tell you! Even in my own room can I have no peace? Must I be dogged even in my dreams by shameless and unscrupulous females? Oh, unfortunate youth that I am!

ASENATH. (*setting her candle down on the table*) Now I know what is the matter with you, Joseph! You have an obsession.

JOSEPH. What is an obsession?

ASENATH. Don't you know what an obsession is? (She sits down on the stool at the end of the table). Haven't you heard of the great wizard in the land of the barbarians who explains everything by a new magic?

JOSEPH. Is he the author of that popular new dream-book?

ASENATH. Yes. All Egypt is mad on the subject of dreams. Everybody, from Pharaoh to the fiddler's wife, is telling about his latest dream, or listening to some one else tell his.

JOSEPH. (*sitting down on the other stool*) Speaking of dreams, I had a curious one just before you came in.

ASENATH. Did you, Joseph? Tell it to me.

She leans across the table.

JOSEPH. I dreamed--that I saw a dragon with many heads. And each head had the face of a beautiful woman. I was frightened. But I took up a sword and struck. And all the heads except one were severed. All except one. And this one had upon it a crown of iron and a crown of gold. And then the dragon took the crowns from its head, and offered them to me! I did not know what to do. . . . And then I awoke.

ASENATH. Shall I interpret your dream for you, Joseph? The dragon with the many heads signifies the women of Egypt, who are all in love with you. The one that remains when you have struck off the rest, is the one who will succeed where all the others have failed. The crown of iron signifies power. The crown of gold, riches. She offers them to you. . .

JOSEPH. (*leaning forward*) Asenath--do you really think it means--

ASENATH. (*coldly*) I really think it means that you have a persecution--mania. You imagine that every woman you meet has designs on you. . . . I suppose you think that *I* came here to make love to you?

JOSEPH. No, my dear Asenath. I know better than that. When young women come to my room at midnight, it is only to borrow a book to read--or to ask my advice about their personal affairs. I know, because they tell me so. Which did you come for--a book, or advice?

ASENATH. Neither. I came to give a book to you--and to give you some advice.... Do you remember telling me, once in Heliopolis, that the man who knew enough about the climate of Egypt to predict a famine could make himself the richest man in the kingdom? Well--here is everything you want to know, in an old book I found in my father's library in Heliopolis. This is the book I came to give you.

She holds out a scroll.

JOSEPH. (*taking it*) Dear Asenath--

ASENATH. (*interrupting him*) And now the advice. It is this. Ally yourself to the wisest woman in the land of Egypt--one who can teach you to interpret the dreams of Pharaoh. Then you shall become the second in power in the kingdom.

JOSEPH. The second in power in the kingdom! Asenath--do not mock me. Can you do this?

ASENATH. I swear that I can and will!

JOSEPH. (*overcome*) You do love me....

ASENATH. (*jumping up*) Love you! What nonsense! (*Scornfully*) Love!

JOSEPH. You--you don't love me?

ASENATH. Not in the least!

JOSEPH. But--but--then what are you doing it for?

ASENATH. I am doing it for *myself*. Do you think I wish to stay in Heliopolis all my life? No--I want power and riches--and I intend to have them. But I cannot get them, unfortunately, without wasting my time with some man.

JOSEPH. And I--?

ASENATH. You are the man.

JOSEPH. Admirable!

ASENATH. Hate me if you will--

JOSEPH. On the contrary! (*He goes toward her*.) Wonderful creature!

ASENATH. (*retreating*) What do you say?

JOSEPH. I say that you are a woman after my own heart. (He holds out his arms. She retreats to the other end of the table.) I did not think that there existed in all the world a woman as profoundly egoistic, as unscrupulously ambitious, as myself. You are my true mate. Come, we shall rule Egypt together!

ASENATH. (*in front of the table*) Am I to understand that this is a strictly business proposition?

JOSEPH. No. It is a declaration of love. I adore you! I desire you! I cannot live without you!

ASENATH. Please don't be silly.

JOSEPH. (*hurt*) Is it possible that you do not believe in my love?

ASENATH. It is a little difficult. . . .

JOSEPH. You think that I am a hard man--and so I am. But when I look at you, I tremble and grow weak. My knees are become as water, and the blood roaring in my veins confuses me.

ASENATH. Can I, a mere woman, so disturb you?

JOSEPH. You have more than a mere woman's beauty. Your hands are lotus petals. Your eyes are silver fireflies mirrored in a pool. Your breasts are white birds nestling behind the leaves of a pomegranate tree.

ASENATH. You have a smooth tongue, Joseph! One would think you really were in love at last. . . .

JOSEPH. I love you more than anything else in the world. You mean more to me than power, more than riches, more than freedom itself.

ASENATH. I could almost believe that you are in earnest. . . .

JOSEPH. Tell me, O lovely creature for whom my soul and body thirst, how can I prove my sincerity? What proof can I give you?

ASENATH. You can give me--that ring!

She points to the ring which Potiphar has given him.

JOSEPH. (*looking at her, then at the ring, takes it off, saying*)-- Freedom!

He puts it on her finger. He draws her toward him. She resists. The candle is knocked over, and all is darkness.

ASENATH. (*in the darkness, faintly*) Joseph! Joseph!

THE ANGEL INTRUDES

A COMEDY

To GEORGE CRAM COOK

"The Angel Intrudes" was first produced by the Provincetown Players, New York City, in 1917, with the following cast:

The Policeman...... Abram Gillette
The Angel.......... James Light
Jimmy Pendleton.... Justus Sheffield
Annabelle.......... Edna St. Vincent Millay

Washington Square by moonlight. A stream of Greenwich Villagers hurrying across to the Brevoort before the doors are locked. In their wake a sleepy policeman.

The policeman stops suddenly on seeing an Angel with shining garments and great white wings, who has just appeared out of nowhere.

THE POLICEMAN. Hey, you!

THE ANGEL. (*haughtily, turning*) Sir! Are you addressing me?

THE POLICEMAN. (*severely*) Yes, an' I've a good mind to lock you up.

THE ANGEL. (*surprised and indignant*) How very inhospitable! Is that the way you treat strangers?

THE POLICEMAN. Don't you know it's agen the law of New York to parade the streets in a masquerade costume?

THE ANGEL. No. I didn't know. You see, I've just arrived this minute from Heaven.

THE POLICEMAN. Ye look it. (*Taking his arm kindly*) See here, me lad, you've been drinkin' too many of them stingers. Ye'd better take a taxi and go home.

THE ANGEL. What! So soon?

THE POLICEMAN. I know how ye feel. I've been that way meself. But I can't leave ye go traipsin' about in skirts.

THE ANGEL. (*drawing away*) Sir, I'm not traipsing about. I am attending to important business, and I must ask you not to detain me.

THE POLICEMAN. (*suspiciously*) Not so fast, me laddie-buck. What business have you at this hour of the night? Tell me that.

THE ANGEL. I don't mind telling you. It concerns a mortal called James Pendleton.

THE POLICEMAN. (*genial again*) Aha! So you're a friend of Jimmy Pendleton's, are you?

THE ANGEL. Not exactly. I am his Guardian Angel.

THE POLICEMAN. Well, faith, he needs one! Come, me b'y, I'll see ye safe to his door.

THE ANGEL. Thank you. But, if you don't mind, I prefer to go alone.

He turns away.

THE POLICEMAN. Good night to you, then.

 He idly watches the angelic figure walk away, and then stares with amazement as it spreads its wings and soars to the top of Washington Arch. Pausing there a moment, it soars again in the air, and is seen wafting its way over the neighbouring housetops to the northeast. The policeman shakes his head in disapproval.

Jimmy Pendleton is dozing in an easy chair before the grate-fire in Ms studio in Washington Mews. A yellow-backed French novel has fallen from his knee to the floor. It is Anatole France's "La Revolte des Anges". A suitcase stands beside the chair. Jimmy is evidently about to go on some journey.

A clock begins to strike somewhere. Jimmy Pendleton awakes.

JIMMY. What a queer dream! (*He looks at his watch*.) Twelve o'clock. The taxi ought to be here. (He takes two tickets from his pocket, looks at them, and puts them back. Then he commences to pace nervously up and down the room, muttering to himself)--Fool! Idiot! Imbecile! (He is not, so that you could notice it, any of these things. He is a very handsome man of forty. There is the blast of an auto-horn outside. He makes an angry gesture.) Too late! That's the taxi. (But he stands uncertainly in the middle of the floor. There is a loud pounding on the knocker.) Yes, yes!

He makes a movement toward the door, when it suddenly opens, and a lovely lady enters. He stares at her in surprise.

JIMMY. Annabelle!

Annabelle is little. Annabelle's petulant upturned lips are rosebud red. Annabelle's round eyes are baby-blue. Annabelle is--young.

ANNABELLE. Yes! It's me! (There is a tiny lisp in Annabelle's speech.) I got tired of waiting, and the door was unlocked, so I came right in.

JIMMY. Well!

ANNABELLE. (*hurt*) Aren't you glad to see me?

JIMMY. I'm--delighted. But--but--I thought we were to meet at the station.

ANNABELLE. So we were.

JIMMY. You haven't changed your mind?

ANNABELLE. No. . . .

JIMMY. Er--good.

ANNABELLE. But--

JIMMY. Yes--?

ANNABELLE. I got to wondering. . . . (She drifts to the easy chair in front of the fire.)

JIMMY. Wondering . . . about what? (*He looks at his watch*.)

ANNABELLE. About love. . . .

JIMMY. Well . . . (*He lights a cigarette*)--it's a subject that can stand a good deal of wondering about. I've wondered about it myself.

ANNABELLE. That's just it--you speak so cynically about it. I don't believe you're in love with me at all!

JIMMY. Nonsense! Of course I'm in love with you.

ANNABELLE. (*sadly*) No you're not.

JIMMY. (*angrily*) But I tell you I am!

ANNABELLE. No. . . .

JIMMY. Foolish child!

ANNABELLE. Well, let's not quarrel about it. We'll talk about something else.

JIMMY. (*vehemently*) What do you suppose this insanity is if it is not love? What do you imagine leads me to this preposterous escapade, if not that preposterous passion?

ANNABELLE. That isn't the way *I* love you.

JIMMY. Then why do you come with me?

ANNABELLE. Perhaps I'm not coming.

JIMMY. Yes you are. It's foolish--mad--wicked--but you're coming. (*She begins to cry softly*.) If not--ten minutes away is safety and peace and comfort. Shall I call a taxi for you? (She shakes her head.) No, I thought not. Oh, it's love all right. . . . Antony and Cleopatra defying the Mann Act! Romance! Beauty! Adventure! How can you doubt it?

ANNABELLE. I hate you!

JIMMY. (*cheerfully*) I don't mind. (*Smiling*) I rather hate you myself. And that's the final proof that this is love.

ANNABELLE. (*sobbing*) I thought love was something quite--different!

JIMMY. You thought it was beautiful. It isn't. It's just blithering, blathering folly. We'll both regret it tomorrow.

ANNABELLE. *I* Won't!

JIMMY. Yes you will. It's human nature. Face the facts.

ANNABELLE. (*tearfully*) Facing the facts is one thing and being in love is another,

JIMMY. Quite so. Well, how long do you think your love for me will last?

ANNABELLE. For ever!

JIMMY. H'm! I predict that you will fall in love with the next man you meet.

ANNABELLE. I think you're perfectly horrid.

JIMMY. So do I. I disapprove of myself violently. I'm a doddering lunatic, incapable of thinking of anything but you. I can't work. I can't eat, I can't sleep. I'm no use to the world. I'm not a man, I'm a mess. I'm about to do something silly because I can't do anything else.

ANNABELLE. (*pouting*) You've no respect for me.

JIMMY. None whatever. I love you. And I'm going to carry you off.

ANNABELLE. You're a brute.

JIMMY. Absolutely. I'd advise you to go straight home.

ANNABELLE. (*defiantly*) Perhaps I shall!

JIMMY. Then go quick. (*He takes out his watch*.) In one minute, if you are still here, I shall pick you up and carry you off to South America.--Quick! there's the door!

ANNABELLE. (*faintly*) I--I want to go. . . .

JIMMY. Well, why don't you? . . . Thirty seconds!

ANNABELLE. I--I can't!

JIMMY. (*shutting his watch*) Time's up. The die is cast! (He lifts her from the chair. She clings to him helplessly.) My darling! My treasure! My beloved!--Idiot that I am!

He kisses her fiercely.

ANNABELLE. (*struggling in his arms*) No! No! No! Stop!

JIMMY. Never!

ANNABELLE. Stop! Please! Please! Oh! . . .

 The light suddenly goes out, and an instant later blazes out again, revealing the Angel, who has suddenly arrived in the middle of the room. The two of them stare at the apparition.

THE ANGEL. (*politely*) I hope I am not intruding?

JIMMY. Why--why--not exactly!

ANNABELLE. (*in his arms, indignantly*) Jimmy! who is that man?

JIMMY. (*becoming aware of her and putting her down carefully*) I--why--the fact is, I don't--

THE ANGEL. The fact is, madam, I am his Guardian Angel.

ANNABELLE. An Angel! Oh!

THE ANGEL. Tell me, *have* I intruded?

ANNABELLE. No, not at all!

THE ANGEL. Thank you for reassuring me. I feared for a moment that I had made an inopportune entrance. I was about to suggest that I withdraw until you had finished the--er--ceremony--which I seem to have interrupted.

JIMMY. (*surprised*) But wasn't that what you came for--to interrupt?

THE ANGEL. I beg your pardon!

JIMMY. (*bewilderedly*) I mean--if you are my Guardian Angel, and all that sort of thing, you *must* have come to--to interfere!

THE ANGEL. I hope you will not think I would be capable of such presumption.

JIMMY. (*puzzled*) You don't want to--so to speak--reform me?

THE ANGEL. Not at all. Why, I scarcely know you!

JIMMY. But you're my--my Guardian Angel, you say?

THE ANGEL. Ah, yes, to be sure. But the relation of angelic guardianship has for some hundreds of years been a purely nominal one. We have come to feel that it is best to allow mortals to attend to their own affairs.

JIMMY. (*abruptly*) Then what did you come for?

THE ANGEL. For a change. One becomes tired of familiar scenes. And I thought that perhaps my relationship to you might serve in lieu of an introduction. I wanted to be among friends.

JIMMY. Oh--I see.

ANNABELLE. Of course. We're delighted to have you with us. Won't you sit down? (*She leads the way to the fire*.)

THE ANGEL. (*perching on back of one of the big chairs*) If you don't mind! My wings, you know.

JIMMY. (*hesitantly*) Have a cigarette?

THE ANGEL. Thank you. (*He takes one*.) I am most anxious to learn the more important of your earthly arts and sciences. Please correct me if I go wrong. This is my first attempt, remember. He blows out a puff of smoke.

ANNABELLE. (*from the settle*) You're doing it very nicely.

THE ANGEL. It is incense to the mind.

ANNABELLE. (*laughing, blowing a series of smoke rings*) You must learn to do it like this!

THE ANGEL. (*in awe*) That is too wonderful an art. I fear I can never learn it!

ANNABELLE. I will teach you.

THE ANGEL. (*earnestly*) If you were my teacher, I think I could learn anything.

ANNABELLE. (*giggles charmingly*).

JIMMY. (*embarrassed*) Really, Annabelle...!

ANNABELLE. What's the matter?

JIMMY. Ordinarily I wouldn't mind your flirting with strangers, but...

ANNABELLE. (*indignantly*) Jimmy! How can you?

THE ANGEL. It was my fault, I'm sure--if fault there was. But what is it--to flirt? You see, I wish to learn everything.

ANNABELLE. I hope you never learn that.

THE ANGEL. I put myself in your hands.

JIMMY. Er--would you like a--drink?

THE ANGEL. Thank you. I am very thirsty. (*Taking the glass*.) This is very different from what we have in Heaven. (He tastes it. A look of gratified surprise appears on his face.) And much better! (He drains the glass and hands it back.) May I have some more?

ANNABELLE. Be careful!

THE ANGEL. What should I be careful of?

ANNABELLE. Don't drink too much of that--if it's the first time.

THE ANGEL. Why not? It is an excellent drink.

JIMMY. (*laughing*) The maternal instinct! She is afraid you may make yourself--ridiculous.

THE ANGEL. Angels do not care for appearances. (He stands up magnificently in the chair, towering above them.) Besides . . . (*refilling his glass*) I feel that you do an injustice to this drink. Already it has made a new being of me. (He looks at Annabelle.) I feel an emotion that I have never known before. If I were in heaven, I should sing.

ANNABELLE. Oh! Won't you sing?

THE ANGEL. The fact is, I know nothing but hymns. And I'm tired of

them. That was one reason why I left heaven. And this robe. . . .
(*He descends to the floor, viewing his garment with disapproval*.)
Have you an extra suit of clothes you could lend me?

JIMMY. (*reflectively*) Yes, I think I have some things that might
fit. (*The Angel waits*.) Do you want them now? I'll look.

He goes into the bedroom. . . . The Angel looks at Annabelle until
his gaze becomes insupportable, and she covers her eyes. Then he comes
over to her side.

THE ANGEL. (*gravely*) I am very much afraid of you. (He takes her
hands in his.)

ANNABELLE. (*smiling*) One would never guess it!

THE ANGEL. I am more afraid of you than I was of God. But even though I
fear you, I must come close to you, and touch you. I feel a strange,
new emotion like fire in my veins. This world has become beautiful to
me because you are in it. I want to stay here so that I may be with
you. . . .

ANNABELLE. (*shaken, but doubting*) For how long?

THE ANGEL. For ever. . . .

ANNABELLE. (*in his arms*) Darling!

THE ANGEL. I am so ignorant! There is something I want to do right now,
only I do not know how to go about it properly.

He bends shyly toward her lips.

ANNABELLE. I will teach you.

She kisses him.

THE ANGEL. Heaven was nothing to this. They kiss again. . . . Enter Jimmy, with an old suit of clothes over his arm. He pauses in dumbfounderment. At last he regains his voice.

JIMMY. Well! *They look up. Neither of them is perturbed.*

THE ANGEL. (*blandly*) Has something happened to annoy you? (*Jimmy shakes the clothes at him in an outraged gesture.*) Oh, my new costume. Thank you so much!

He takes the clothes from Jimmy, and examines them with interest.

JIMMY. (*bitterly, to Annabelle*) I suppose I've no right to complain. You can make love to anybody you like. In fact, now that I come to think of it, I predicted this very thing. I said you'd fall in love with the next man you met. So it's off with the old love, and--

ANNABELLE. (*calmly*) I have never been in love before.

JIMMY. The fickleness of women is notorious. It is exceeded only by their mendacity. But Angels have up to this time stood in good repute. Your conduct, sir, is scandalous. I am amazed at you.

THE ANGEL. It may be scandalous, but it should not amaze you. It has happened too often before. I could quote you many texts from learned theological works. "And the sons of God looked at the daughters of men and saw that they were fair." But even if it were as unusual as you imagine, that would not deter me.

JIMMY. You are an unscrupulous wretch. If these are the manners of Heaven, I am glad it is so far away, and means of communication so difficult. A few more of you would corrupt the morals of five continents. You are utterly depraved--Here! what are you doing?

THE ANGEL. I am taking off my robes, so as to put on my new clothes.

JIMMY. Spare the common decencies at least. Go in the other room.

THE ANGEL. Certainly, if that is the custom here. With the clothes over his arm, he goes into the bedroom.

JIMMY. (*sternly, to Annabelle*) And now tell me, what do you mean by this?

ANNABELLE. (*simply*)--We are in love.

JIMMY. Do you mean to say you would throw me over for that fellow?

ANNABELLE. Why not?

JIMMY. What good is he? All he can do is sing hymns. In three months he'll be a tramp.

ANNABELLE. I don't care. And he won't be a tramp. I'll look after him.

JIMMY. (*sneeringly*) The maternal instinct! Well, take care of him if you like. But of course you know that in six weeks he'll fall in love with somebody else?

ANNABELLE. No he won't. I'm sure that I am the only girl in the world to him.

JIMMY. Of course you're the only girl in the world to him--now. You're the only one he's ever seen. But wait till he sees the others! Six weeks? On second thought I make it three days. Immortal love! (He laughs.)

ANNABELLE. What difference does it make? You don't understand. Whether it lasts a day or a year, while it lasts it will be immortal.
The Angel enters, dressed in Jimmy's old clothes, and carrying his wings in his hands. He seems exhilarated.

THE ANGEL. How do I look?

JIMMY. It is customary to wear one's tie tucked inside the vest.

THE ANGEL. (flinging the ends of the gorgeous necktie over his shoulder) No! Though I have become a man, I do not without some regret put on the dull garb of mortality. I would not have my form lose all its original brightness. Even so it is the excess of glory obscured.

ANNABELLE. (*coming over to him*) You are quite right, darling.

She tucks the tie inside his vest.

THE ANGEL. Thank you, beloved.--And now these wings! Take them, and burn them with your own sweet hands, so that I can never leave you, even if I would.

ANNABELLE. No! I would rather put them away for you in a closet, so that you can go and look at them any time you want to, and see that you have the means to freedom ready to your hand. I shall never hold you against your will. I do not want to burn your wings. I really don't! But if you insist--!

She takes the wings, and approaches the grate.

JIMMY. (*to the Angel*) Don't let her do it! Fool! You don't know what you are doing. Listen to me! You think that she is wonderful--superior--divine. It is only natural. There are moments when I have thought so myself. But I know why I thought so, and you have yet to learn. Keep your wings, my friend, against the day of your awakening--the day when the glamour of sex has vanished, and you see in her, as you will see, an inferior being, with a weak body, a stunted mind, devoid of creative power, almost devoid of imagination, utterly lacking in critical capacity--a being who does not know how to work, nor how to talk, nor even how to play!

 Annabelle, dropping the wings on the hearth, stares at him, in speechless anger.

THE ANGEL. Sir! Do you refer in these vulgar and insulting terms to the companion of my soul, the desire of my heart, the perfect lover whose lips have kindled my dull senses to ecstasy?

JIMMY. I do. Remember that I know her better than you do, young man. Take my advice and leave her alone. Even now it is not too late! Save yourself from this folly while there is still time!

THE ANGEL. Never!

JIMMY. Then take these tickets--and I hope that I never see either of you again! He holds out the tickets. Annabelle, after a pause, steps forward and takes them.

ANNABELLE. That is really sweet of you, Jimmy! The blast of an auto-horn is heard outside.

JIMMY. (*bitterly*) And there's my taxi. Take that, too.

THE ANGEL. Farewell!

He opens the door. Annabelle, at his side, turns and blows Jimmy a kiss. Stonily, Jimmy watches them go out. Then he picks up his suitcase and goes, with an air of complete finality, into the other room.

There is a moment's silence, and then the door opens softly, and the Angel looks in, enters surreptitiously, seizes up the wings, and with them safely clasped to his bosom, vanishes again through the door.

LEGEND

A ROMANCE

TO KIRAH MARKHAM

"Legend" was first produced, under the title, "My Lady's Mirror," at the Liberal Club, in 1915, with the following cast:

He .... Clement Wood
She.............. Kirah Markham

A small room with a little table in the centre, and a chair on either side of it. At the back is the embrasure of a French window opening on a balcony. In another wall is the outer door. The room is lighted by tall candles. There is an image of the Virgin in a niche in the corner.

HE. (a cloaked figure, standing with hat and stick in one hand and holding in the other a large square parcel) First of all, I have a present for you.

SHE. (*where she has just risen when he entered*) A present! Oh, thank you, Luciano!

HE. It is not me you have to thank for this present! (He puts it on the table.) It is some one else. I am only the bearer.

SHE. Who can it be? Who would send me a present?

HE. What a question, Donna Violante! Not a man in Seville, not a man in Spain, but would send you gifts if he dared. It is not "Who would?" but "Who could?"

SHE. No man, as you know, Luciano, has that right.

HE. Have you so soon forgotten your husband, Violante? He, surely, has that right! And it is thoughtful of him, too, to pause in the midst of his antiquarian researches in Rome, to think of his young wife and send her a gift. He appreciates you more than I imagined. Under his grizzled and scientific exterior, he is a human being. I respect him for it.

He puts down his hat and stick.

SHE. My husband! But why, then, do *you* bring it?

HE. I was commissioned by him to do so. I received the package, this morning, with a letter. Shall I read it to you?

He takes out the letter.

SHE. Yes.... But why should he not send it direct to *me*?

HE. Your husband is a man of curious and perverse mind, Violante, and, in spite of his interest in dead things, not without some insight into the living soul. I think it gave him an obscure pleasure to think of *me* the bearer of *his* gift. But shall we let him speak for himself?

He opens the envelope.

SHE. Yes. Read the letter.

She sits down to listen.

HE. (*reading*) "My dear young friend: I am sending you a package, which I beg you, as a favour, to deliver to Donna Violante, my wife. It contains a gift of an unusual sort, which you as well as she will appreciate. As you know, it is the unusual which interests me--the unusual and the old. And yet, antiquarian though I am, I flatter myself that I understand the mind of a beautiful young woman, especially when that young woman is my wife. I have found her a mirror. Yes, a mirror! Under this name it seems commonplace enough, but when you have seen it I do not think you will say so. It is not the kind of mirror that is ordinarily found in a lady's boudoir. Yet it will give to her a faithful reflection of her loveliness as it is in truth. I found it-- this will interest you--in the Catacombs. You would not think the early Christians had so much vanity! Yet it was a mirror into which the virgin-martyrs-to-be of the time of Nero looked each day. As they looked, let Donna Violante look. Say to her from me--'Look long and well into this mirror, and profit by what you see.'--Humbly your friend, Don Vincenzio." . . . Is not that a pleasant letter?

He restores the letter to his pocket.

SHE. There is something in it that makes me shiver.... Let us look.

She takes the paper from the box and is about to open it when he stops her.

HE. No. Not now. I want to talk to you.

SHE (*lapsing into a hostile coldness*) Yes.

HE. You know what I have to say. I have said it so often. I shall say it once more.

SHE. (*appealingly*) Luciano!

HE. No, let me speak. You are not happy. You do not love your husband. And you are too young and beautiful to live without love.

SHE. Please!

HE. I love you. And you love me. Why do you not surrender yourself to love?

SHE. Why do you say such things? They hurt me.

HE. They are reality. Does reality hurt you? Are you living in a shadow-world, that you should flinch from the hard touch of truth? I say it again. I love you.

SHE. Before you started to talk like that, we were so happy together.

HE. Before I spoke out the truth of my own heart and yours. You didn't want it spoken out. You didn't want to be told you were in love. It was a thing too harsh and sweet. It frightened you to think of. You wanted us to sit for ever, like two lovers painted on a fan, fixed in an everlasting and innocuous bliss.

SHE. Well, you have succeeded in spoiling that. You have made me unhappy, if that gives you any pleasure.

HE. It was not I who have spoiled your shadow-world. It is love, coming like the dawn on wings of flame, and shattering the shadows with spears of gold. It is love that has made you unhappy. You tremble at its coming, and try to flee. But the day of love has come for you.

SHE. Ah, if it had only come before--before....

HE. Before you married that perverse old man. If it had come while you were still a maiden, free, with a right to give yourself up to it! Ah, you would have given yourself gloriously! It is beautiful--but it is a dream, and the time calls for a deed. We love each other. We can take our happiness now. Will you do it? Will you come away with me?

SHE. No.

HE. Then I if you cannot take your happiness, give me mine. If you cannot be a woman, be an angel, and lean down from your dream heaven to slake my earthly thirst.

SHE. No.

HE. No angel? Then a goddess! You want to be worshipped. You want to be adored. I will worship you, but not from afar, I will adore you in my own fashion. I will praise you without words, and you shall be the answer to my prayer. Will you?

SHE. No.

HE. "No." "No." "No." How did your lips learn to say that word so easily? They are not made to say such a word. They are too young, too red, to say "No" to Life. When you say that word, the world grows black. The stars go out, the leaves wither, the heart stops beating. It is a word that kills. It is the word of Death. Dare you say it again? Answer me, do we love each other? . . . Silence.

SHE. I think . . . I am going . . . to cry.

HE. And tears. Tears are a slave's answer. Speak. Defend yourself. Why do you stay here? Why do you deny yourself happiness? Why won't you come with me?

SHE. I cannot.

HE. Always the same phrase that means nothing. Ah, Violante, lady of few words, you know how to baffle argument. If I could only make you speak! If I could only see what the thoughts are that darken your will!

SHE. Don't.

HE. By God! I wonder that I don't hate you instead of love you. There is something ignobly feminine about you. You are incapable of action-- almost incapable of speech. Your lips are shut tight against kisses, and when they open to speak, all that they say is "Don't."

SHE. What do you expect to gain by scolding me?

HE. I gain the satisfaction of telling you the truth--that you have the most cowardly soul that was ever belied by a glorious body. Who would think to look at you that you were afraid?

SHE. It's no use bullying me.

HE. I know that, Violante. It's the poorest way to woo a woman. But I have tried every other way. I have pleaded, and been answered with silence. I have wooed you with caresses, and been answered with tears.

SHE. I am sorry, Luciano.

HE. I want you to be glad.

SHE. I am glad--glad of you--in spite of everything.

HE. Gladness is something fiercer than that. You are too tame. Oh, if I could reach and rouse your soul!

SHE. My soul is yours already....

HE. And your body...?

SHE. It is impossible.

HE. No. It isn't impossible. But I'll tell you what is impossible. This--for me to go on loving you and despising you.... I came here today to make one last appeal to you. I don't mean it as a threat. But I am going away tonight for ever--with you, or without you. You must decide.

SHE. (*rising*) But--I don't want you to go, Luciano!

HE. You will miss me, I know. But don't think too much of that. You will find a new friend--if you decide against me.

SHE. And I must decide now?

HE. Yes--now.

SHE. But how can I? Oh, Luciano!

HE. I know it is hard. But I will not make it harder. Violante: I have sought to appeal to your emotion when my appeal to your will was in vain. But tonight I will leave you to make your own decision. You must come to me freely or not at all. There must be no regrets.

SHE. I cannot do it.

HE. If you say that when I return I will accept it as a final answer. I am going out on the balcony--for a long minute. And while I am gone you must decide what to do. Will you?

SHE. Yes.

HE. (*turning at the window*) And if while I am gone you wish to recall my arguments to your mind--(he points to the box on the table)--look in your mirror there. Your beauty will plead for me. As Don Vincenzio said: Look long and well into that mirror, lady, and profit by what you see.

He goes out. . . . She looks after him, and when he is gone holds out her arms towards the door. She makes a step towards it, and then stops, her hands falling to her sides. Her head droops for a moment or two, and then is slowly lifted. Her eyes sweep the room imploringly, and rest on the image of the Virgin. She goes over to it and kneels.

SHE. Mary, Mother of God, give me a sign. I do not know what to do. Help me. I must decide. Love has entered my heart, and it may be that I cannot be a good woman any longer. You will be kind to me, and pity me, and send me a sign. Perhaps you will let me have my lover, for you are kind.

She crosses herself, rises, and looks around. She sees the box on the table, and puts her hand to her face with a gesture of sudden thought. She smiles.

Perhaps that is the sign!

She goes to the box and touches it.

He said it would plead for him. . . .

She opens it--and starts back with a gesture and a cry.

It *is* the sign!

With one hand over her heart she approaches it again. She takes out of the box and puts on the table a skull. . . . She stares at it a long while, and then turns with a shiver.

How cold it is here! Where are the lights?

She is compelled to look again.

I had never thought of death. My heart is cold, too. The chill of the grave is on me. Was I ever in love? It seems strange to remember. What is his name? I almost have forgotten. And he is waiting for me. I will show him this. We should have looked at it together. . . .

A silence, as her mood changes.

So *he* had planned it! He wanted to cast the chill of the grave upon our love. He saw it all as though he had been here. He sent us-- this! How well he knew me--better than I knew myself. An old man's cunning! To stop my pulses throbbing with love, and put out the fever in my eyes. A trick! Yes, but it suffices. One look into the eyeless face of Death turns me to ashes. I am no longer fit for love. . . .

She turns to the door.

Why does he not come for his answer?

She looks for a lingering moment toward the door, and then turns
back again to the table. Her mood changes again.

A present from a husband to a wife!

She takes it up in her hands.

A lady's mirror! What was it that he said? "Look long and well into
this mirror, and profit by what you see," My mirror from the Catacombs!

She sinks into a chair, holding it between her hands as it rests on
the table. Her tone is trance-like.

I look. I see the end of all things. I see that nothing matters. Is
that your message? Why do you grin at me? You laugh to think that my
face is like your face--or will be soon--in a few years-tomorrow. You
mock at me for thinking I am alive. I am dead, you say. Dead, like you.
Am I?

She rises.

No. Not yet. For a moment--a little lifetime--I have life, I Have lips
and eyelids made for kisses. I have hands that burn to give caresses,
and breasts that ache to take them. I have a body made to suffer the
deep stings of love. This flesh of mine shall be a golden web woven of
pain and joy.

She takes up the skull again.

You were alive once, and a virgin-martyr? You denied yourself love? You
sent away your lover? No wonder you speak so plainly to me now. Back,
girl, to your coffin!

She puts the skull in the box, and closes the lid softly. She turns to the door and waits. At last he enters.

HE. (*dejected*) You have--decided?

SHE. Yes. I have decided.

HE. I knew. It is no use. I will go.

He turns to the door.

SHE. Wait! (*He turns back incredulously*.) I have decided to go with you. (*He stands stock-still*.) Don't you understand? Take me. I am yours. Don't you believe it?

HE. Violante!

SHE. It is hard to believe, isn't it. I have been a child. Now I am a woman. And shall I tell you how I became a woman? (She points to the box on the table.) I looked in my mirror there. I saw that I was beautiful--and alive. Tell me, am I not beautiful--and alive?

HE. There is something terrible about you at this moment. I am almost afraid of you.

SHE. Kiss me, Luciano!

SWEET-AND-TWENTY

A COMEDY

To EDNA ST. VINCENT MILLAY

"Sweet-and-Twenty" was first produced by the Provincetown Players, New York City, in 1918, with the following cast:

The Young Woman .... Edna St. Vincent
Millay The Young Man ... Ordway Tead
The Agent .... Otto Liveright
The Guard .... Louis Ell

The cherry-orchard scene was effectively produced on a small stage by a blue-green back-drop with a single conventionalized cherry-branch painted across it, and two three-leaved screens masking the wings, painted in blue-green with a spray of cherry blossoms.

 A corner of the cherry orchard on the country place of the late Mr. Boggley, now on sale and open for inspection to prospective buyers. The cherry orchard, now in full bloom, is a very pleasant place. There is a green-painted rustic bench beside the path. . . .

A young woman, dressed in a light summer frock and carrying a parasol, drifts in from the back. She sees the bench, comes over to it and sits down with an air of petulant weariness.

A handsome young man enters from the right. He stops short in surprise on seeing the charming stranger who lolls upon the bench. He takes off his hat.

HE. Oh, I beg your pardon!

SHE. Oh, you needn't! I've no right to be here, either.

HE. (*coming over to her*) Now what do you mean by that?

SHE. I thought perhaps you were playing truant, as I am.

HE. Playing truant?

SHE. I was looking at the house, you know. And I got tired and ran away.

HE. Well, to tell the truth, so did I. It's dull work, isn't it?

SHE. I've been upstairs and down for two hours. That family portrait gallery finished me. It was so old and gloomy and dead that I felt as if I were dead myself. I just had to do something. I wanted to jab my parasol through the window-pane. I understood just how the suffragettes felt. But I was afraid of shocking the agent. He is such a meek little man, and he seemed to think so well of me. If I had broken the window I would have shattered his ideals of womanhood, too, I'm afraid. So I just slipped away quietly and came here.

HE. I've only been there half an hour and we--I've only been in the basement. That's why our tours of inspection didn't bring us together sooner. I've been cross-examining the furnace. Do you understand furnaces? (*He sits down beside her*) I don't.

SHE. Do you like family portraits? I hate 'em!

HE. What! Do the family portraits go with the house?

SHE. No, thank heaven. They've been bequeathed to some museum, I am told. They're valuable historically--early colonial governors and all that sort of stuff. But there is some one with me who--who takes a deep interest in such things.

HE. (*frowning at a sudden memory*) Hm. Didn't I see you at that real estate office in New York yesterday?

SHE. Yes. *He* was with me then.

HE. (*compassionately*) I--I thought I remembered seeing you with--with him.

SHE. (*cheerfully*) Isn't he *just* the sort of man who would be interested in family portraits?

HE. (*confused*) Well--since you ask me--

SHE. Oh, that's all right. Tubby's a dear, in spite of his funny old ideas. I like him very much.

HE. (*gulping the pill*) Yes....

SHE. He's so anxious to please me in buying this house. I suppose it's all right to have a house, but I'd like to become acquainted with it gradually. I'd like to feel that there was always some corner left to explore--some mystery saved up for a rainy day. Tubby can't understand that. He drags me everywhere, explaining how we'll keep this and change that--dormer windows here and perhaps a new wing there.... I suppose you've been rebuilding the house, too?

HE. No. Merely decided to turn that sunny south room into a study. It would make a very pleasant place to work. But if you really want the place, I'd hate to take it away from you.

SHE. I was just going to say that if *you* really wanted it, *I'd* withdraw. It was Tubby's idea to buy it, you know--not mine. You *do* want it, don't you?

HE. I can't say that I do. It's so infernally big. But Maria thinks I ought to have it. (*Explanatorily*)--Maria is--

SHE. (*gently*) She's--the one who is interested in furnaces. I understand. I saw her with you at the real-estate office yesterday. Well--furnaces are necessary, I suppose. (There is a pause, which she breaks suddenly.) Do you see that bee?

HE. A bee?

He follows her gaze up to a cluster of blossoms.

SHE. Yes--there! (*Affectionately*)--The rascal! There he goes.

Their eyes follow the flight of the bee across the orchard. There is a silence. Alone together beneath the blossoms, a spell seems to have fallen upon them. She tries to think of something to say--and at last succeeds.

SHE. Have you heard the story of the people who used to live here?

HE. No; why?

SHE. The agent was telling us. It's quite romantic--and rather sad. You see, the man that built this house was in love with a girl. He was building it for her--as a surprise. But he had neglected to mention to her that he was in love with her. And so, in pique, she married another man, though she was really in love with him. The news came just when he had finished the house. He shut it up for a year or two, but eventually married some one else, and they lived I here for ten years--most unhappily. Then they went abroad, and the house was sold. It was bought, curiously enough, by the husband of the girl he had been in love with. They lived here till they died-hating each other to the end, the agent says.

HE. It gives me the shivers. To think of that house, haunted by the memories of wasted love! Which of us, I wonder, will have to live in it? I don't want to.

SHE. (*prosaically*) Oh, don't take it so seriously as all that. If one can't live in a house where there's been an unhappy marriage, why, good heavens, where is one going to live? Most marriages, I fancy, are unhappy.

HE. A bitter philosophy for one so young and--

SHE. Nonsense! But listen to the rest of the story. The most interesting part is about this very orchard.

HE. Really!

SHE. Yes. This orchard, it seems, was here before the house was. It was part of an old farm where he and she--the unhappy lovers, you know-- stopped one day, while they were out driving, and asked for something to eat. The farmer's wife was busy, but she gave them each a glass of milk, and told them they could eat all the cherries they wanted. So they picked a hatful of cherries, and ate them, sitting on a bench like this one. And then he fell in love with her. . . .

HE. And . . . didn't tell her so. . . .

She glances at him in alarm. His self-possession has vanished. He is pale and frightened, but there is a desperate look in his eyes, as if some unknown power were forcing him to do something very rash. In short, he seems like a young man who has just fallen in love.

SHE. (*hastily*) So you see this orchard is haunted, too!

HE. I feel it. I seem to hear the ghost of that old-time lover whispering to me. . . .

SHE. (*provocatively*) Indeed! What does he say?

HE. He says: "I was a coward; you must be bold. I was silent; you must speak out."

SHE. (*mischievously*) That's very curious--because that old lover isn't dead at all. He's a Congressman or Senator or something, the Agent says.

HE. (*earnestly*) It's all the same. His youth is dead; and it is his youth that speaks to me.

SHE. *quickly* You mustn't believe all that ghosts tell you.

HE. Oh, but I must. For they know the folly of silence--the bitterness of cowardice.

SHE. The circumstances were--slightly--different, weren't they?

HE. (*stubbornly*) I don't care!

SHE. (*soberly*) You know perfectly well it's no use.

HE. I can't help that!

SHE. Please! You simply mustn't! It's disgraceful!

HE. What's disgraceful?

SHE. (*confused*) What you are going to say.

HE. (*simply*) Only that I love you. What is there disgraceful about that? It's beautiful!

SHE. It's wrong.

HE. It's inevitable.

SHE. Why inevitable? Can't you talk with a girl in an orchard for half an hour without falling in love with her?

HE. Not if the girl is you.

SHE. But why especially *me*?

HE. I don't know. Love--is a mystery. I only know that I was destined to love you.

SHE. How can you be so sure?

HE. Because you have changed the world for me. It's as though I had been groping about in the dark, and then--sunrise! And there's a queer feeling here. (*He puts his hand on his heart*.) To tell the honest truth, there's a still queerer feeling in the pit of my stomach. It's a gone feeling, if you must know. And my knees are weak. I know now why men used to fall on their knees when they told a girl they loved her; it was because they couldn't stand up. And there's a feeling in my feet as though I were walking on air. And--

SHE. (*faintly*) That's enough!

HE. And I could die for you and be glad of the chance. It's perfectly absurd, but it's absolutely true. I've never spoken to you before, and heaven knows I may never get a chance to speak to you again, but I'd never forgive myself if I didn't say this to you now. I love you! love you! love you! Now tell me I'm a fool. Tell me to go. Anything--I've said my say. . . . Why don't you speak?

SHE. I--I've nothing to say--except--except that I--well--(almost inaudibly) I feel some of those symptoms myself.

ME. (*triumphantly*) You love me!

SHE. I--don't know. Yes. Perhaps.

HE. Then kiss me!

SHE. (*doubtfully*) No. . . .

HE. Kiss me!

SHE. (*tormentedly*) Oh, what's the use?

HE. I don't know. I don't care. I only know that we love each other.

SHE. (*after a moment's hesitation, desperately*) I don't care, either! I do want to kiss you.

She does. . . . He is the first to awake from the ecstasy.

HE. It is wrong--

SHE. (*absently*) Is it?

HE. But, oh heaven! kiss me again! (*She does.*)

SHE. Darling!

HE. Do you suppose any one is likely to come this way?

SHE. No.

HE. (*speculatively*) Your husband is probably still in the portrait gallery....

SHE. My husband! (*Drawing away*) What do you mean? (Thoroughly awake now) You didn't think--? (She jumps up and laughs convulsively.) You thought poor old Tubby was my husband?

HE. (*staring up at her bewildered*) Why, isn't he your husband?

SHE. (*scornfully*) No!! He's my uncle!

HE. Your unc--

SHE. Yes, of course! (*Indignantly*) Do you suppose I would be married to a man that's fat and bald and forty years old?

HE. (*distressed*) I--I beg your pardon. I did think so.

SHE. Just because you saw me with him? How ridiculous!

HE. It was a silly mistake. But--the things you said! You spoke so--realistically--about marriage.

SHE. It was your marriage I was speaking about. (With hasty compunction) Oh, I beg your--

HE. My marriage! (*He rises*.) Good heavens! And to whom, pray, did you think I was married? (*A light dawning*) To Maria? Why, Maria is my aunt!

SHE. Yes--of course. How stupid of me.

HE. Let's get this straight. Are you married to *anybody*?

SHE. Certainly not. As if I would let myself be made love to, if I were a married woman!

HE. Now don't put on airs. You did something quite as improper. You made love to a married man.

SHE. I didn't.

HE. It's the same thing. You thought I was married.

SHE. But you aren't.

HE. No. I'm not married. And--and--*you're* not married. (The logic of the situation striking him all of a sudden) In fact--! *He pauses, rather alarmed*.

SHE. Yes?

HE. In fact--well--there's no reason in the world why we *shouldn't* make love to each other!

SHE. (*equally startled*) Why--that's so!

HE. Then--then--shall we?

SHE. (*sitting down and looking demurely at her toes*) Oh, not if you don't want to!

HE. (*adjusting himself to the situation*) Well--under the circumstances--I suppose I ought to begin by asking you to marry me. .

SHE. (*languidly, with a provoking glance*) You don't seem very anxious to.

HE. (*feeling at a disadvantage*) It isn't that--but--well--

SHE. (*lightly*) Well what?

HE. Dash it all, I don't know your name!

SHE. (*looking at him with mild curiosity*) That didn't seem to stop you a while ago....

HE. (*doggedly*) Well, then--will you marry me?

SHE. (*promptly*) No.

HE. (*surprised*) No! Why do you say that?

SHE. (*coolly*) Why should I marry you? I know nothing about you. I've known you for less than an hour.

HE. (*sardonically*) That fact didn't seem to keep you from kissing me.

SHE. Besides--I don't like the way you go about it. If you'd propose the same way you made love to me, maybe I'd accept you.

HE. All right. (**Dropping on one knee before her**) Beloved! (An awkward pause) No, I can't do it. (He gets up and distractedly dusts off his knees with his handkerchief.) I'm very sorry.

SHE. (*with calm inquiry*) Perhaps it's because you don't love me any more?

HE. (*fretfully*) Of course I love you!

SHE. (*coldly*) But you don't want to marry me.... I see.

HE. Not at all! I do want to marry you. But--

SHE. Well?

HE. Marriage is a serious matter. Now don't take offense! I only meant that-well--(**He starts again**.) We *are* in love with each other, and that's the important thing. But, as you said, we don't know each other.

I've no doubt that when we get acquainted we will like each other better still. But we've got to get acquainted first.

SHE. (*rising*) You're just like Tubby buying a house. You want to know all about it. Well! I warn you that you'll never know all about me. So you needn't try.

HE. (*apologetically*) It was *your* suggestion.

SHE. (*impatiently*) Oh, all right! Go ahead and cross-examine me if you like. I'll tell you to begin with that I'm perfectly healthy, and that there's no T. B., insanity, or Socialism in my family. What else do you want to know?

HE.(*hesitantly*) Why did you put in Socialism, along with insanity and T. B.?

SHE. Oh, just for fun. You aren't a Socialist, are you?

HE. Yes. (*Earnestly*) Do you know what Socialism is?

SHE. (*innocently*) It's the same thing as Anarchy, isn't it?

HE. (*gently*) No. At least not my kind. I believe in municipal ownership of street cars, and all that sort of thing. I'll give you some books to read.

SHE. Well, I never ride in street cars, so I don't care whether they're municipally owned or not. By the way, do you dance?

HE. No.

SHE. You must learn right away. I can't bother to teach you myself, but

I know where you can get private lessons and become really good in a month. It is stupid not to be able to dance.

HE. (*as if he had tasted quinine*) I can see myself doing the tango! Grr!

SHE. The tango went out long ago, my dear.

HE. (*with great decision*) Well--I *won't* learn to dance. You might as well know that to begin with.

SHE. And I won't read your old books on Socialism. You might as well know that to begin with!

HE. Come, come! This will never do. You see, my dear, it's simply that I *can't* dance, and there's no use for me to try to learn.

SHE. Anybody can learn. I've made expert dancers out of the awkwardest men!

HE. But, you see, I've no inclination toward dancing. It's out of my world.

SHE. And I've no inclination toward municipal ownership. *It's* out of *my* world!

HE. It ought not to be out of the world of any intelligent person.

SHE. (*turning her back on him*) All right--if you want to call me stupid!

HE. (*turning and looking away meditatively*) It appears that we have very few tastes in common.

SHE. (*tapping her foot*) So it seems.

HE. If we married we might be happy for a month--

SHE. Perhaps.

They remain with their backs to each other.

HE. And then--the old story. Quarrels. . . .

SHE. I never could bear quarrels. . . .

HE. An unhappy marriage. . . .

SHE. (*realizing it*) Oh!

HE. (*hopelessly turning toward her*) I can't marry you.

SHE. (*recovering quickly and facing him with a smile*) Nobody asked you, sir!

HE. (*with a gesture of finality*) Well--there seems to be no more to say.

SHE. (*sweetly*) Except good-bye.

HE. (*firmly*) Good-by, then.

He holds out his hand.

SHE. (*taking it*) Good-bye!

HE. (*taking her other hand--after a pause, helplessly*) Good-bye!

SHE. (*drowning in his eyes*) Good-bye!

 They cling to each other, and are presently lost in a passionate embrace. He breaks loose and stamps away, then turns to her.

HE. Damn it all, we *do* love each other!

SHE. (*wiping her eyes*) What a pity that is the only taste we have in common!

HE. Do you suppose that is enough?

SHE. I wish it were!

HE. A month of happiness--

SHE. Yes!

HE. And then--wretchedness,

SHE. No--never!

HE. We mustn't do it.

SHE. I suppose not.

HE. Come, let us control ourselves.

SHE. Yes, let's (*They take hands again* .)

HE. (*with an effort*) I wish you happiness. I--I'll go to Europe for a year. Try to forget me.

SHE. I shall be married when you get back--perhaps.

HE. I hope it's somebody that's not bald and fat and forty. Otherwise--!

SHE. And you--for goodness sake! marry a girl that's very young and very, very pretty. That will help.

HE. We mustn't prolong this. If we stay together another minute--

SHE. Then go!

HE. I can't go!

SHE. You must, darling! You must!

HE. Oh, if somebody would only come along!

They are leaning toward each other, dizzy upon the brink of another kiss, when somebody does come--a short, mild-looking man in a derby hat. There is an odd gleam in his eyes.

THE INTRUDER. (*startled*) Excuse me!

They turn and stare at him, but their hands cling fast to each other.

SHE. (*faintly*) The Agent!

THE AGENT. (*in despairing accents*) Too late! Too late!

THE YOUNG MAN. No! Just in time!

THE AGENT. Too late, I say! I will go.

He turns away.

THE YOUNG MAN. No! Stay!

THE AGENT. What's the use? It has already begun. What good can I do now?

THE YOUNG MAN. I'll show you what good you can do now. Come here! (*The Agent approaches*.), Can you unloose my hands from those of this young woman?

THE YOUNG WOMAN. (*haughtily, releasing herself and walking away*) You needn't trouble! I can do it myself.

THE YOUNG MAN. Thank you. It was utterly beyond my power. (To the Agent)--Will you kindly take hold of me and move me over there? (*The Agent propels him away from the girl*.) Thank you. At this distance I can perhaps say farewell in a seemly and innocuous manner.

THE AGENT. Young man, you will not say farewell to that young lady for ten days-and perhaps never!

THE YOUNG WOMAN. What!

THE AGENT. They have arranged it all.

THE YOUNG MAN. *Who* have arranged *what*?

THE AGENT. Your aunt, Miss Brooke--and (*to the young woman*) your uncle, Mr. Egerton--

The young people turn and stare at each other in amazement.

THE YOUNG MAN. Egerton! Are you Helen Egerton?

HELEN. And are you George Brooke?

THE AGENT. Your aunt and uncle have just discovered each other up at the house, and they have arranged for you all to take dinner together tonight, and then go to a ten-day house-party at Mr. Egerton's place on Long Island. (*Grimly*) The reason of all this will be plain to you. They want you two to get married.

GEORGE. Then we're done for! We'll have to get married now whether we want to or not!

HELEN. What! Just to please *them*? I shan't do it!

GEORGE. (*gloomily*) You don't know my Aunt Maria.

HELEN. And Tubby will try to bully me, I suppose. But I won't do it--no matter what he says!

THE AGENT. Pardon what may seem an impertinence, Miss; but is it really true that you don't want to marry this young man?

HELEN. (*flaming*) I suppose because you saw me in his arms--! Oh, I want to, all right, but--

THE AGENT. (*mildly*) Then what seems to be the trouble?

HELEN. I--oh, you explain to him, George.

She goes to the bench and sits down.

GEORGE. Well, it's this way. As you may have deduced from what you saw, we are madly in love with each other--

HELEN. (*from the bench*) But I'm not madly in love with municipal ownership. That's the chief difficulty.

GEORGE. No, the chief difficulty is that I refuse to entertain even a platonic affection for the tango.

HELEN. (*irritably*) I told you the tango had gone out long ago!

GEORGE. Well, then, the maxixe.

HELEN. Stupid!

GEORGE. And there you have it! No doubt it seems ridiculous to you.

THE AGENT. (*gravely*) Not at all, my boy. I've known marriage to go to smash on far less than that. When you come to think of it, a taste for dancing and a taste for municipal ownership stand at the two ends of the earth away from each other. They represent two different ways of taking life. And if two people who live in the same house can't agree on those two things, they'd disagree on a hundred things that came up every day. And what's the use for two different kinds of beings to try to live together? It doesn't work, no matter how much, love there is between them.

GEORGE. (rushing up to him in surprise and gratification, and shaking his hand warmly) Then you're on our side! You'll help us not to get married!

THE AGENT. Your aunt is very set on it--and your uncle, too, Miss!

HELEN. We must find some way to get out of it, or they'll have us cooped up together in that house before we know it. (Rising and coming over to the Agent) Can't you think up some scheme?

THE AGENT. Perhaps I can, and perhaps I can't. I'm a bachelor myself, Miss, and that means that I've thought up many a scheme to get out of marriage myself.

HELEN. (*outraged*) You old scoundrel!

THE AGENT. Oh, it's not so bad as you may think, Miss. I've always gone through the marriage ceremony to please them. But that's not what I call marriage.

GEORGE. Then what *do* you call marriage?

HELEN. Yes, I'd like to know!

THE AGENT. Marriage, my young friends, is an iniquitous arrangement devised by the Devil himself for driving all the love out of the hearts of lovers. They start out as much in love with each other as you two are today, and they end by being as sick of the sight of each other as you two will be five years hence if I don't find a way of saving you alive out of the Devil's own trap. It's not lack of love that's the trouble with marriage--it's marriage itself. And when I say marriage, I don't mean promising to love, honour, and obey, for richer, for poorer, in sickness and in health till death do you part--that's only human nature to wish and to attempt. And it might be done if it weren't for the iniquitous arrangement of marriage.

GEORGE. (*puzzled*) But what is the iniquitous arrangement?

THE AGENT. Ah, that's the trouble! If I tell you, you won't believe me.

You'll go ahead and try it out, and find out what all the unhappy ones have found out before you. Listen to me, my children. Did you ever go on a picnic? (He looks from one to the other--they stand astonished and silent.) Of course you have. Every one has. There is an instinct in us which makes us go back to the ways of our savage ancestors--to gather about a fire in the forest, to cook meat on a pointed stick, and eat it with our fingers. But how many books would you write, young man, if you had to go back to the campfire every day for your lunch? And how many new dances would *you* invent if you lived eternally in the picnic stage of civilization? No! the picnic is incompatible with everyday living. As incompatible as marriage.

GEORGE. But--

HELEN. But--

THE AGENT. Marriage is the nest-building instinct, turned by the Devil himself into an institution to hold the human soul in chains. The whole story of marriage is told in the old riddle: "Why do birds in their nests agree? Because if they don't, they'll fall out." That's it. Marriage is a nest so small that there is no room in it for disagreement. Now it may be all right for birds to agree, but human beings are not built that way. They disagree, and home becomes a little hell. Or else they do agree, at the expense of the soul's freedom stifled in one or both.

HELEN. Yes, but tell me--

GEORGE. Ssh!

THE AGENT. Yet there *is* the nest-building instinct. You feel it, both of you. If you don't now, you will as soon as you are married. If you are fools, you will try to live all your lives in a love-nest; and you will imprison your souls within it, and the Devil will laugh.

HELEN. (*to George*) I am beginning to be afraid of him.

GEORGE. So am I.

THE AGENT. If you are wise, you will build yourselves a little nest secretly in the woods, away from civilization, and you will run away together to that nest whenever you are in the mood. A nest so small that it will hold only two beings and one thought--the thought of love. And then you will come back refreshed to civilization, where every soul is different from every other soul--you will let each other alone, forget each other, and do your own work in peace. Do you understand?

HELEN. He means we should occupy separate sides of the house, I think. Or else that we should live apart and only see each other on week-ends. I'm not sure which.

THE AGENT. (*passionately*) I mean that you should not stifle love with civilization, nor encumber civilization with love. What have they to do with each other? You think you want a fellow student of economics. You are wrong. *You* think you want a dancing partner. You are mistaken. You want a revelation of the glory of the universe.

HELEN. (*to George, confidentially*) It's blithering nonsense, of course. But it *was* something like that--a while ago.

GEORGE. (*bewilderedly*) Yes; when we knew it was our first kiss and thought it was to be our last.

THE AGENT. (*fiercely*) A kiss is always the first kiss and the last--or it is nothing.

HELEN. (*conclusively*) He's quite mad.

GEORGE. Absolutely.

THE AGENT. Mad? Of course I am mad. But--

He turns suddenly, and subsides as a man in a, guard's uniform enters.

THE GUARD. Ah, here you are! Thought you'd given us the slip, did you? (*To the others*) Escaped from the Asylum, he did, a week ago, and got a job here. We've been huntin' him high and low. Come along now!

GEORGE. (*recovering with difficulty the power of speech*) What--what's the matter with him?

THE GUARD. Matter with him? He went crazy, he did, readin' the works of Bernard Shaw. And if he wasn't in the insane asylum he'd be in jail. He's a bigamist, he is. He married fourteen women. But none of 'em would go on the witness stand against him. Said he was an ideal husband, they did. Fourteen of 'em! But otherwise he's perfectly harmless.

THE AGENT. (*pleasantly*) Perfectly harmless! Yes, perfectly harmless!

He is led out.

HELEN. That explains it all!

GEORGE. Yes--and yet I feel there was something in what he was saying.

HELEN. Well--are we going to get married or not? We've got to decide that before we face my uncle and your aunt.

GEORGE. Of course we'll get married. You have your work and I mine, and--

HELEN. Well, if we do, then you can't have that sunny south room for a study. I want it for the nursery.

GEORGE. The nursery!

HELEN. Yes; babies, you know!

GEORGE. Good heavens!

A LONG TIME AGO

A TRAGIC FANTASY

TO BROR NORDFELDT

"A Long Time Ago" was first produced by the Provincetown Players, New York City, in 1917, with the following cast:

The Old Woman .... Miriam Kiper
The Fool.................... Duncan MacDougal
The Queen.................. Ida Rauh
The Sailor.................. George Cram Cook
The Prince.................. Pendleton King

The courtyard of a palace. On one side, broad steps, and a door, leading to the palace. On the other, steps leading downward. At the back, a rose-arbour, and in front of it a wide seat.

On the steps before the door a fool is sitting, plucking at a musical instrument. On the lower steps stands an old woman, richly dressed.

THE OLD WOMAN. Why do you sit there, fool, and twang at that harp?

There's no occasion for making music. Nobody has been winning any battles. How long has it been since a great fight was heard of?

THE FOOL. If there had been a battle, old woman, they would have had to get some one besides myself to celebrate the winning of it. I do not like fighting.

THE OLD WOMAN. What does a scrawny little weakling like you know of fighting, and why should you have an opinion?

THE FOOL. The days of fighting are over, and a good thing it is, too. Four kingdoms we have about us, that in the bloody old days we would be for ever marching against, and they against us, killing and burning and destroying the crops till a quiet man would be sick to think of it. But that's all past. Twenty years we have been at peace with them, and that's ever since the young queen was born, and I hope it may last as long as she lives.

THE OLD WOMAN. There's no stopping a fool when he starts to talk. But it is right you are that the good old days are gone. Those were the days of great heroes, like the father of her that is now Queen. They were fine men that stood beside him, and one was my own man. I said to him, "This is the time a brave man is sure to be killed. If you come back to me, I'll always think you were a coward." He died along with a thousand of the best men in the kingdom fighting around the King. That was a great day. Four kingdoms at once we fought, and beat them to their knees. Glad enough they were to make peace with the child of that dead king.

THE FOOL. Spare me, woman. I've heard that old story often enough. What do you suppose all that fighting was for, if it wasn't to put an end to quarrelling for all time? If the old King was alive now, he'd sit in his palace and drink his ale and listen to music, and when he saw the young men giving kisses to the young women under the trees he'd be glad enough. But you still go cawing for blood, like an old crow.

THE OLD WOMAN. I'll not talk to such a one. You can see with your own eyes that our enemies are strong and prosperous. We let them into the kingdom with their silks and their satins and their jewels to sell. They walk about the city here and laugh to themselves, thinking how they will spoil and destroy everything soon. It may be this year, it may be next year. If the old King were alive, he'd never have let them get half so strong. He would have kept them in fear of us, and trained up a fine band of heroes, too, making raids on them once in a while. There's the city that shoves itself right up against our borders--I can see our men coming home from the spoiling of it, all red with spilt wine and blood. . . .

THE FOOL. You're a disgusting old woman. If I hear any more of that talk, I'm likely to slap the face of you, even if you are the Queen's nurse. Go away before you spoil my afternoon.

THE OLD WOMAN. I could speak to the Queen and have you beaten, do you know that?

THE FOOL. Woman, go away. I do not want to be bothered by the old and the garrulous. I am composing a love-song.

THE OLD WOMAN. Has any one ever loved you, I would like to know? Now if
it were that young prince who is staying with us, he would have some right to make love-songs--if what they say is true, that every woman he meets on his journey falls in love with him. Even our own Queen, I am thinking. But only three days does he stay in any place, and then he is up and gone on his long journey that nobody understands the reason or the end of, from the east to the west. He is too wise to be held by

such toys as love.

THE FOOL. Then he is more a fool than I.

THE OLD WOMAN. Who should know about love, if not a man who has been
loved by many women and by great queens? But you, what do you know
about it?

THE FOOL. The trouble with the old is that they forget so many things.
I am sorry for you, woman. You think yourself wise, but the fool that
sits at the Queen's doorstep and looks at her as she passes, and she
never seeing him at all, is wiser than you.

THE OLD WOMAN. I have wasted enough words with you. I will go away and
sit in the sun and think of the days when there were heroes.

She goes.

THE FOOL. And I will make a song about love. I will make a song about
the love that is too high for pride and too deep for shame.

The door has opened, and the young Queen stands looking down at him.

THE QUEEN. What is that, fool? What are the words you are saying?

THE FOOL. (*kneeling*) I was speaking of a love that is too high
for pride and too deep for shame.

THE QUEEN. And whose love is that, fool?

THE FOOL. It is the love of all who really love, and it is the only love worth making a song about.

THE QUEEN. (*smiling*) And how do you come to be so wise as to know about such things?

THE FOOL. I know because I am a fool.

THE QUEEN. I am well answered. And you are not the only fool in the world, I am thinking. But tell me, fool, have you seen any of the Prince's men here?

THE FOOL. No, but I have heard that the ship is being got ready for sailing. . . .

THE QUEEN. (*rebukingly*) I did not ask you that. (She is about to go, but turns back, and gives him a piece of money.) This is for you to buy wine with and get drunken. You are not amusing when you are sober. (*She starts to go, but turns again*.) Fool, do you believe in magic?

THE FOOL. I have heard that the old wizard who lives in a cave down by the shore is able to rouse storms and keep vessels from sailing.....

THE QUEEN. (*looking at him, for a moment fixedly*) I have a great mind to have you poisoned. Here, take this, and remember that I said to be drunken.

She gives him another piece of money, and goes off by way of the rose-trellised passage-way. A sailor comes up the steps.

THE SAILOR. Fool, where is the Prince?

THE FOOL. I do not know, sailor, but I can tell you what I think.

THE SAILOR. What difference does it make what you think? I have a message to deliver to him.

THE FOOL. I think that the Queen has sung him to sleep, and that he has not yet awakened.

THE SAILOR. It is likely enough. But I have been sent by the captain, and I must see him.

THE FOOL. You look hot.

THE SAILOR. I am so hot and thirsty that I could drink a barrelful of wine. It is well enough for the Prince to lie about and eat and drink and be sung to by pretty women, but we sailors have work to do. This business of staying only three days in each port disgusts me. No sooner do we get ashore than we have to go back on board again. I saw a girl yesterday, a beauty, and not afraid of a man. There must be many like that here, but what good does it do me? I spent all my money on her, and now I can't even get a drink. It's a shame.

THE FOOL. Would you like a drink?

THE SAILOR. Fool, don't make a mock of my thirst, or I'll twist your neck.

THE FOOL. Look at this. (***Shows him a coin***.)

THE SAILOR. What a piece of luck! Is it real money? Where did you get it?

THE FOOL. Your prince gave it to me, and said I was to treat any of his sailors that I came across.

THE SAILOR. Then it's all right. Why didn't you say so before? Come along. If you were as thirsty as I am--!

They go down the steps. The door opens, and the Prince comes out. He looks up and down.

THE PRINCE. And now begins again my long journey from the east to the west. . . .

The old woman appears.

THE OLD WOMAN. Well, have you waked at last?

THE PRINCE. You are a bitter-tongued old woman. But for all that, I think you are my friend. Perhaps the only friend I have here.

THE OLD WOMAN. You are right. For all that you sleep your holiday away, you are a brave man. And I am the only one in this kingdom that thinks well of bravery. The rest want to smother it with kisses.

THE PRINCE. True enough. I feel that already I am becoming soft. Never before have I been unwilling to leave a city--

THE OLD WOMAN. Or a Queen. . . .

THE PRINCE. I must go on board ship. Is it ready, I wonder? The captain promised to send word to me. . . .

THE OLD WOMAN. Yes, it is time you went, before they have made a lap-dog
of you.

THE PRINCE. You speak very freely. Are you not afraid of the Queen?

THE OLD WOMAN. She does not know what she is doing. She has grown up in
a base time of peace, and she does not understand that it is not a
man's business to sleep and drink wine and exchange kisses with pretty
queens. She would turn you from your purpose--

THE PRINCE. My purpose? What do you know of my purpose?

THE OLD WOMAN. I have not guessed your secret. But I know that you are
not merely taking a pleasure journey. I have seen heroes, and you have
the eyes of one. The end of all this journeying from the east to the
west is something great and terrible--and I will not have you turned
aside.

THE PRINCE. Something great and terrible....Yes....

THE OLD WOMAN. You have the look of one who does not care for rest or
peace or the love of a woman for more than a day. But there is a
weakness in you, too. If you would go, go quickly.

THE PRINCE. I wonder why the sailor does not come. It looks like a
storm.

The sky has become ominously dark.

THE OLD WOMAN. Would a storm hold you back?

THE PRINCE. Is that what you think of me, old woman?

THE OLD WOMAN. Well, we shall see what stuff you are made of....

She shuffles off. The Queen enters.

THE QUEEN. (*coming up to him, tenderly*) When did you wake?

THE PRINCE. Did you think your voice had enough magic in it to make me sleep till you returned? We have just time to say farewell.

THE QUEEN. There is a storm coming up. Do you see how black the sky is?

THE PRINCE. I am not afraid of storms.

THE QUEEN. Of course you are not afraid of storms. Did you think you had to prove your bravery?

THE PRINCE. The three days are over.

THE QUEEN. And how quickly!

THE PRINCE. I told you I could stay only three days.

THE QUEEN. I thought you were a king, and could do whatever you chose....

THE PRINCE. I have chosen to stay only three days.

THE QUEEN. In what way have I offended you?

THE PRINCE. I made my choice long ago, before I knew you.

THE QUEEN. And now you are afraid to change your mind?

THE PRINCE. Do you think a brave man changes his mind for pleasure's sake?

THE QUEEN. Forgive me. If it is your happiness to go on, to what end I do not know, I will let you. I do not wish to make you unhappy. But I would give you something to take with you, one more flower of my garden, an unfading rose that shall be like a bright memory of me in your heart always. Will you take it?

She leads him back into the palace. The sailor enters, supported by the fool.

THE SAILOR. (*drunkenly*) Where--where is my Prince? I have a message for him.

THE FOOL. So you said. But you haven't finished telling me about that girl. Her eyes were blue, you said.

THE SAILOR. Blue, yes. If I said blue, then blue it was. Or maybe green, or grey. Maybe I'm. thinking of the hussy back in the last port we stopped at. It's all the same. Reminds me of a little song. Shall I sing you a little song?

THE FOOL. Another song? Sing away then.

THE SAILOR. First another drink from this flagon. Ah! Now I'm ready. I've often been complimented on my voice. (*Sings*)

  We'll go no more a-roving-

No, that's not the one. Let me see. Ah, now I've got it. Listen.
(*Sings*)

  Blue eyes, grey eyes, green-and-gold eyes,
  Eyes that question, doubt, deny,
  Sudden-flashing, cold, hard, bold eyes,
  Here's your answer: I am I!

Not for you, and not for any,
Came I into this man's town--
Barkeep, here's my golden penny,
Come who will and drink it down!

I'm not one to lend and borrow,
I'm not one to overstay--
I shall go alone tomorrow
Whistling, as I came today.

Leave my sword alone, you hussy!
There is blood upon the blade--
Dragon-slaying is a messy
Sort of trade. Put back the blade!

Take my knee and--O you darling!
A man forgets how sweet you are!
Snarling dragons--flowing flagons--
Devil take the morning star!

THE FOOL. Bravo!

THE SAILOR. And there you are! If I do say it myself, I have as good a time as the Prince does. One girl's as nice as another--and maybe nicer, at that. What's a Queen? Can she kiss better than any other girl? I've wondered a bit about it. And the conclusion I've come to is... the conclusion I've come to...

THE FOOL. The conclusion you've come to is--?

THE SAILOR. Right you are. Give me that flagon. That's the stuff. What was I saying? The conclusion I've come to is that the Prince can't have any more fun in three days than any other man. Queen or no Queen. Am I right? Tell me, am I right?

THE FOOL. I wouldn't contradict you....

THE SAILOR. No. Of course you wouldn't. You're a good fellow. You're my friend. Where's that flagon? Ah! And now it's your turn to sing. Sing that little song you sang a while ago. That was a good one. You sing almost as well as I do.

THE FOOL. (*chants*)

In this harsh world and old
Why must we cherish
Fires that grow not cold
In hearts that perish?

With the strong floods of hate
I cleansed my bosom,
But springeth soon and late
The fiery blossom.

What though some lying tale
The mind dissembles?
The scarlet lip turns pale,
The strong hand trembles....

THE SAILOR. No, no, not that one! That one hasn't any tune to it, and it isn't about girls. It's no song at all. I meant the one--you know-- about the young widow. How did it go? (*He swigs from the flagon*.) But I mustn't forget the Prince. Where's that Prince?

THE FOOL. Oh, yes, the Prince. Of course. We mustn't forget the Prince. Come along with me. (He leads the sailor off through the rose-arbour.

The door of the palace opens, disclosing the Prince and the Queen.)

He clasps her hands and then descends the steps.

THE QUEEN. Wait!

She runs down, and tenderly embraces him.

THE PRINCE. Farewell.

THE QUEEN. Must you go?

THE PRINCE. I shall remember you always.

THE QUEEN. (*bitterly*) I suppose that is enough. . . .

They come down the steps together.

THE PRINCE. What is that you say?

THE QUEEN. I say that it is enough that you should think of me sometimes on your long journey from the east to the west. To be remembered--that is the portion of women.

THE PRINCE. You knew what manner of man I was, and that I would not be detained. Why, if you must have the taste of kisses on your lips always, did you not turn to some man of your own land, who would not stray from your side? Why did you give your love to one you had never seen before, and will never see again? I did not ask that you love me. What you gave, I took.

THE QUEEN. I regret nothing that I have given. But I am sorry for you, because you do not understand.

THE PRINCE. It may be that I do not understand. But I know that I may not stay longer in this place. Would you ask me to do otherwise?

THE QUEEN. I would not ask you, no. If you understood, I would have no need of asking. If all things in your life have not changed colour and significance--if I have been to you but as a harlot to one of your sailors,--then leave me.

THE PRINCE. (*confusedly*) It is not true that nothing has changed. My mind is in a turmoil. I am dizzy, I cannot see. I have almost forgotten why I set my heart on this journey. You have bewitched me, and that is why I fear you. If I stay here with you any longer, I shall forget everything. I must go.

THE QUEEN. (*her arms about him*) You have forgotten the meaning of your journey. You will not go.

THE PENCE. I am going. . . .

But he allows himself to be led to the arbour seat.

THE QUEEN. It is too late. You are mine, now, mine for ever. It was for this that you came hither--I am the meaning of your journey. It was ordained that you love me. You must not think of anything else.

THE PRINCE. Why have you done this to me? Are you a witch? I am afraid of you!

He rises.

THE QUEEN. I will teach you strange and terrible secrets.

THE PRINCE. I fear you and yet I trust you. What will come of this I do not know. But I care for nothing. Nothing in the world means anything to me now except you. Why is it that I seem to hate you?

He seizes her and holds her fiercely.

THE QUEEN. That is because you love me at last.

THE PRINCE. I could kill you.

THE QUEEN. You seek in vain to escape love.

The sailor staggers in, sees the Prince, and stops.

THE SAILOR. I am bidden to tell you--

THE PRINCE. Be off!--What is it you say?

The Queen stands still, with her hands over her face.

THE SAILOR. The ship is ready.

THE PRINCE. Go!

The sailor walks away.

THE QUEEN. (*looking after him*) A word, and you have forgotten me already. A moment ago I thought you loved me. Now I am nothing to you.

THE PRINCE. The ship--

THE QUEEN. It is ready to sail. They are waiting for you. Why do you not go?

THE PRINCE. I am sorry. But it is as you say. The ship is ready to sail. I must go.

THE QUEEN. Go quickly.

THE PRINCE. Farewell, then.

THE QUEEN. No, stay. (She throws herself at his feet, and clasps his knees.) See, I beg you to stay. I have no shame left. I beg you. Stay even though you despise me. Stay even though you hate me. I do not care. I will be your slave, your bondwoman. I cannot let you go.

She puts her head in her hands, and weeps.

THE PRINCE. (*looking down at her*) I am sorry. (*After a pause*) Farewell.

He touches her lightly on the shoulder, and, looking toward the sea, leaves her. She rises, and watches him with a stony face until he goes.

The fool enters.

THE QUEEN. Are you drunken, fool, as I bade you be?

THE FOOL. I am drunken, yes, but not with wine. I am drunken with bitterness. With the bitterness of love.

THE QUEEN. Of love, fool?

THE FOOL. With the bitterness of love. It will amuse you, and so I will tell you what I mean. It is you that I love.

THE QUEEN. Life grows almost interesting once more. But are you not afraid that I will have you whipped?

THE FOOL. You would have had me whipped a week ago if I had told you this. But now you will not. Now you know what it is to love. . . .

THE QUEEN. My secrets are on a fool's tongue. But what does it matter? Go on.

THE FOOL. Why did I try to keep the man you love from going away? In the hope that one day I should see you kissing him in the garden, and thus I would be spared the trouble of killing myself. In a word, I am a fool. But I have tried to help you. Why did you not keep him?

THE QUEEN. I have been asking that question of my own heart, fool. I would that I had not come to him a virgin and a Queen, but a light woman skilled in all the ways of love. Then perhaps I could have held him. But now he is gone, and the world is black.

THE FOOL. It is not the world, it is your heart that is black. And it is black with hatred. . . .

THE QUEEN. I think you understand, fool. I would set fire to this palace which the King my father built, I would burn it down tonight, save that it would not make light enough to take away the blackness from my heart.

The sailor again, staggering.

THE QUEEN. What, has the ship not gone?

THE SAILOR. Gone, and left me behind. Gone, and left me. . . .

THE FOOL. Here is still wine in the flagon.

THE SAILOR. Good. Good. Give it to me.

THE QUEEN. (*to the fool*) First bring it to me. (She takes off a ring, and dips it in the wine. To the fool)--I have spoken lightly of poisoning today. Now I think I will try it. I would like to see a man die. It will ease me a little. Come!

The sailor comes and takes it from her hands, while the fool stares fascinated.

THE QUEEN. How does it taste?

THE SAILOR. (*suddenly straightening up, no longer drunk*) Bitter. What was in it?

THE QUEEN. The bitterness of my heart. It will kill you.

THE SAILOR. I have been poisoned. (*He puts his hand to his side*.) I am dying. But first--!

He draws a short sword, and runs at her. The fool starts up, but the Queen motions him away, and waits. When the sailor is almost upon her, he stops, throws up his hands, drops his sword, and falls in a heap.

THE QUEEN. (after a moment, going up, and touching the body with her foot) Dead. So that is what it is like?

THE FOOL. (*trembling*) Do you find it so interesting?

THE QUEEN. No--my heart is already aching with its emptiness again....

What shall I do?

THE FOOL. You might poison me, too. I think I would die in a more original manner than that silly sailor. Yes, I would seize you in my arms and kiss you before I died.

THE QUEEN. That would be amusing. But it is a pity to waste kisses on a dying man. And besides, you are the only one in my kingdom who understands me. I must have you alive to talk to.

THE FOOL. There are strange stories about the kisses of queens.

THE QUEEN. Tell them to me.

THE FOOL. There is an old saying that three kisses bestowed by a queen upon a fool will make a hero of him.

THE QUEEN. That might be interesting. I think I will try it. Come to me, do not be afraid. This day I have given my kisses to a man who thought no more of them than that dead sailor there of the kisses of a harlot. What, must you kneel? Well, then, upon your forehead.

She kisses him upon the forehead as he kneels.

He slowly rises, and as he rises he takes on dignity. His fool's cap is dropped aside, he picks up the dead sailor's sword and girds it on him.

THE QUEEN. Ah, it is true. There is magic in it. You are handsome, too. I am not sorry to have kissed you.

The old woman comes in.

THE QUEEN. Well, what is the news? The ship has sailed, has it not?

THE OLD WOMAN. Straight into the sunset. (She sees the dead man, and looks at the Queen and at the fool.) Who killed him?

THE QUEEN. I killed him. He was left behind, and I do not like to have strangers about.

THE OLD WOMAN. It is a good omen. I have not seen a dead man for twenty
years, save those that died of sickness and old age. When shall we have the good old times when men killed each other with swords? I feel that it is coming. When shall we fall upon the four kingdoms, and tear them to pieces?

THE QUEEN. Ah, that is an idea. That would be something to do.

THE FOOL. Hush your croakings, old woman, and tell us the news that you have come with.

THE OLD WOMAN. How do you know that I come with news? Where is your
cap, fool?

THE FOOL. Speak, or be gone.

THE QUEEN. Beware of this man, for I have been making a hero out of him.

THE OLD WOMAN. Are you mad?

THE QUEEN. Yes, I am mad, so beware of me, too, and tell your news,

THE OLD WOMAN. (*tamed*) It is only that a boat has been seen to put out from the ship, and is coming back to shore.

THE QUEEN. It is doubtless a present for me. The Prince has bethought himself to pay me for my kindness to him. Go, and give orders that any men who are in the boat are to be brought to me, with their hands tied behind them, that I may decide what punishment to inflict upon them. Let it be understood that we do not like strangers in this kingdom.

THE OLD WOMAN. (*grimly*) It shall be as you say.

She goes out.

THE QUEEN. And now I must finish my quaint task. It pleases me to be kissing fools. I think it is becoming a habit of mine. Come to this garden bench, where he and I sat together, and I will kiss you upon the mouth, as I kissed him. Does it hurt you for me to say that? Good. (*They sit down*.) You are the only one in the kingdom who understands me. Lift up your head. (She kisses him. He lifts his head proudly, and sits beside her like a king.) You are silent. Why do you not say something appropriate?

THE FOOL. What I have to say will be with my sword, and your enemies will be the ones to hear it.

THE QUEEN. Ah, I forgot, it is a hero I am making out of you, and all a hero can do is fight. That is a stupid thing. I am sorry now that I kissed you.

THE FOOL. You will not be sorry when I have destroyed your enemies.

THE QUEEN. Now you are beginning to talk like my old nurse. It is well enough to fight, but it should be for amusement, and not with such seriousness. I have only succeeded in making you dull. You were better as a fool.

The Prince enters, with his hands tied behind him, conducted by some soldiers.

THE PRINCE. (*Indignantly*) Why am I treated in this fashion?

THE QUEEN. So it is you?

She looks at him quietly.

THE PRINCE. (*haughtily*) Order that these bonds be taken from my wrists.

THE QUEEN. We do not like strangers in this country. You were tied by my command, and brought here that I might decide what punishment to mete out to you. Look, this was one of your men. (Pointing to the dead body) Carry it away.

The soldiers carry off the body.

THE PRINCE. Are you mad?

THE QUEEN. So it would seem. (*To the fool*) Now cut his bonds.

THE FOOL. He is a brave man, and does not deserve to be treated in this manner.

THE PRINCE. Who are you that you should plead for me? Have I not seen you with a fool's cap?

THE FOOL. And now you see me with a sword.

He cuts the Prince's bonds.

THE PRINCE. Leave us. I wish to speak with the Queen.

THE QUEEN. (*to the fool*) No, stay. (*To the Prince*) It is not
necessary for you to speak. You wish to tell me that the kisses you
had from me were so sweet that you would like to buy some more, and are
willing to put off your journey for a while.

THE PRINCE. I have given up my journey for ever. I know that the only
thing that is real in all the world is love. You are scornful. But I
have neither pride nor shame. I kneel at your feet, and beg you to
forgive me for my folly.

He kneels.

THE QUEEN. It is a pretty speech. But you are too late. I have
forgotten you. While they were tying your hands, I was kissing this man
upon the mouth.

THE PRINCE. (*springing up*) It is a lie!

THE FOOL. Did you say that the Queen lies?

He draws his sword.

THE PRINCE. I do not fight with fools. (*To the Queen*) Send him away,
and have him beaten.

THE QUEEN. Are you not willing to fight with him for me?

THE PRINCE. What do you mean?

THE QUEEN. I mean that I have a new appetite, the appetite for death. I have held myself too lightly, I have gone too willingly to the arms of a chance lover. Now there must be blood to sweeten the kisses.

THE PRINCE. Do you wish this fellow killed?

THE QUEEN. Or you. It makes no difference--not the least. What are my kisses, that I should be careful to whom they go?

THE PRINCE. You speak strangely, and I hardly know you. I have come back as a lover and not as a butcher.

THE QUEEN. My whim has changed--I am in the mood for butchers, now.

THE PRINCE. Say but one word to show that you still love me!

THE QUEEN. I have no word to say.

THE PRINCE. Doubt makes my sword heavy. . . .

THE FOOL. And have you nothing to say to me?

THE QUEEN. You remind me. Come. I must finish what I have begun.

She kisses him on the mouth--the third kiss.

THE PRINCE. (*covering his eyes*) It is I that am mad.

THE FOOL. Come, if you are not afraid.

They go out, the Prince giving one long look at the Queen, whose face remains hard.

It has become a dark twilight.

THE QUEEN. They told me that love was like this--but I laughed, and did not believe.

The old woman comes in.

THE QUEEN. I have sent him out to die.

THE OLD WOMAN. The fool?

THE QUEEN. No, no, no, my lover, my beloved. I tortured him and denied him, and sent him out to die.

THE OLD WOMAN. It is well enough. Death is among us again, and the old times have come back.

There are sounds of fighting, and the women wait in silence. Then the sounds cease, and slowly the soldiers bear in a dead body, which they lay on the steps. They affix torches to either side of the palace door, and go out.

THE FOOL. (going up to the Queen, and holding out his sword to her, hilt-foremost) I have done your bidding, and slain a brave man. Bid some one take this sword and slay me.

THE OLD WOMAN. What a faint heart you are! The fool's cap is on you still. Put back your sword in your scabbard. You will make a soldier yet.

THE QUEEN. You are a brave man. Put back your sword in your scabbard, and may it destroy all my enemies from this day forth.

THE FOOL. What shall I do?

THE QUEEN. I have created you, and now I must give you work to do. You can only fight. Very well, then. Take my soldiers, and lead them to the kingdom that thrusts its chief city against our kingdom's walls. There should be good fighting, and much spoil. When the soldiers have glutted themselves with wine and women, let the city be set on fire. I shall look every night for a light in the sky, and when it comes I shall know it is my bonfire. Perhaps it will light up my heart for a moment. When that is finished, I shall find you other bloody work. Go.

THE FOOL. I understand. You shall have your bonfire. Come, old woman, I want some of your advice.

THE OLD WOMAN. The good old days have come back. Ah, the smell of blood!

They go out.

The queen looks over at the dead man lying on the steps between the torches, and gradually her face softens. She goes over slowly, and kneels by his side, gazing on him. She kisses his mouth, and then rises, goes slowly to the arbour, and sits down. She looks away, and her face becomes hard again.

A sound of trumpets and shouting, the menacing prelude of war, is heard outside.

ENIGMA

A DOMESTIC CONVERSATION

To THEODORE DREISER

"Enigma" was first presented at the Liberal Club, New York City, in 1915.

A man and woman are sitting at a table, talking in bitter tones.

SHE. So that is what you think.

HE. Yes. For us to live together any longer would be an obscene joke. Let's end it while we still have some sanity and decency left.

SHE. Is that the best you can do in the way of sanity and decency--to talk like that?

HE. You'd like to cover it up with pretty words, wouldn't you? Well, we've had enough of that. I feel as though my face were covered with spider webs. I want to brush them off and get clean again.

SHE. It's not my fault you've got weak nerves. Why don't you try to behave like a gentleman, instead of a hysterical minor poet?

HE. A gentleman, Helen, would have strangled you years ago. It takes a man with crazy notions of freedom and generosity to be the fool that I've been.

SHE. I suppose you blame me for your ideas!

HE. I'm past blaming anybody, even myself. Helen, don't you realize that this has got to stop? We are cutting each other to pieces with knives.

SHE. You want me to go. . . .

HE. Or I'll go--it makes no difference. Only we've got to separate, definitely and for ever.

SHE. You really think there is no possibility--of our finding some way?... We might be able--to find some way.

HE. We found some way, Helen--twice before. And this is what it comes to. . . . There are limits to my capacity for self-delusion. This is the end.

SHE. Yes. Only--

HE. Only what?

SHE. It--it seems . . . such a pity. . . .

HE. Pity! The pity is this--that we should sit here and haggle about our hatred. That's all there's left between us.

SHE. (*standing up*) I won't haggle, Paul. If you think we should part, we shall this very night. But I don't want to part this way,

Paul. I know I've hurt you. I want to be forgiven before I go.

HE. (*standing up to face her*) Can't we finish without another sentimental lie? I'm in no mood to act out a pretty scene with you.

SHE. That was unjust, Paul. You know I don't mean that. What I want is to make you understand, so you won't hate me.

HE. More explanations. I thought we had both got tired of them. I used to think it possible to heal a wound by words. But we ought to know better. They're like acid in it.

SHE. Please don't, Paul--This is the last time we shall ever hurt each other. Won't you listen to me?

HE. Go on.

He sits down wearily.

SHE. I know you hate me. You have a right to. Not just because I was faithless--but because I was cruel. I don't want to excuse myself--but I didn't know what I was doing. I didn't realize I was hurting you.

HE. We've gone over that a thousand times.

SHE. Yes. I've said that before. And you've answered me that that excuse might hold for the first time, but not for the second and the third. You've convicted me of deliberate cruelty on that.
And I've never had anything to say. I couldn't say anything, because the truth was; too preposterous. It wasn't any use telling it before. But now I want you to know the real reason.

HE. A new reason, eh?

SHE. Something I've never confessed to you. Yes. It is true that I was cruel to you--deliberately. I did want to hurt you. And do you know why? I wanted to shatter that Olympian serenity of yours. You were too strong, too self-confident. You had the air of a being that nothing could hurt. You were like a god.

HE. That was a long time ago. Was I ever Olympian? I had forgotten it. You succeeded very well--you shattered it in me.

SHE. You are still Olympian. And I still hate you for it. I wish I could make you suffer now. But I have lost my power to do that.

HE. Aren't you contented with what you have done? It seems to me that I have suffered enough recently to satisfy even your ambitions.

SHE. No--or you couldn't talk like that. You sit there--making phrases. Oh, I have hurt you a little; but you will recover. You always recovered quickly. You are not human. If you were human, you would remember that we once were happy, and be a little sorry that all that is over. But you can't be sorry. You have made up your mind, and can think of nothing but that.

HE. That's an interesting--and novel--explanation.

SHE. I wonder if I can't make you understand. Paul--do you remember when we fell in love?

HE. Something of that sort must have happened to us.

SHE. No--it happened to me. It didn't happen to you. You made up your mind and walked in, with the air of a god on a holiday. It was I who fell--headlong, dizzy, blind. I didn't want to love you. It was a force too strong for me. It swept me into your arms. I prayed against it. I had to give myself to you, even though I knew you hardly cared. I had to--for my heart was no longer in my own breast. It was in your hands, to do what you liked with. You could have thrown it in the dust.

HE. This is all very romantic and exciting, but tell me--did I throw it in the dust?

SHE. It pleased you not to. You put it in your pocket. But don't you realize what it is to feel that another person has absolute power over you? No, for you have never felt that way. You have never been utterly dependent on another person for happiness. I was utterly dependent on you. It humiliated me, angered me. I rebelled against it, but it was no use. You see, my dear, I was in love with you. And you were free, and your heart was your own, and nobody could hurt you.

HE. Very fine--only it wasn't true, as you soon found out.

SHE. When I found it out, I could hardly believe it. It wasn't possible. Why, you had said a thousand times that you would not be jealous if I were in love with some one else, too. It was you who put the idea in my head. It seemed a part of your super-humanness.

HE. I did talk that way. But I wasn't a superman. I was only a damned fool.

SHE. And Paul, when I first realized that it might be hurting you--that you were human after all--I stopped. You know I stopped.

HE. Yes--that time.

SHE. Can't you understand? I stopped because I thought you were a person like myself, suffering like myself. It wasn't easy to stop. It tore me to pieces. But I suffered rather than let you suffer. But when

I saw you recover your serenity in a day while the love that I had struck down in my heart for your sake cried out in a death agony for months, I felt again that you were superior, inhuman--and I hated you for it.

HE. Did I deceive you so well as that?

SHE. And when the next time came, I wanted to see if it was real, this godlike serenity of yours. I wanted to tear off the mask. I wanted to see you suffer as I had suffered. And that is why I was cruel to you the second time.

HE. And the third time--what about that?

She bursts into tears, and sinks to the floor, with her head on the chair, sheltered by her arms. Then she looks up.

SHE. Oh, I can't talk about that--I can't. It's too near.

HE. I beg your pardon. I don't wish to show an unseemly curiosity about your private affairs.

SHE. If you were human, you would know that there is a difference between one's last love and all that have gone before. I can talk about the others--but this one still hurts.

HE. I see. Should we chance to meet next year, you will tell me about it then. The joys of new love will have healed the pains of the old.

SHE. There will be no more joy or pain of love for me. You do not believe that. But that part of me which loves is dead. Do you think I have come through all this unhurt? No. I cannot hope any more, I cannot believe. There is nothing left for me. All I have left is regret for

the happiness that you and I have spoiled between us. . . . Oh, Paul, why did you ever teach me your Olympian philosophy? Why did you make me
think that we were gods and could do whatever we chose? If we had realized that we were only weak human beings, we might have saved our happiness!

HE. (*shaken*) We tried to reckon with facts--I cannot blame myself for that. The facts of human nature: people do have love affairs within love affairs. I was not faithful to you. . . .

SHE. (*rising to her feet*) But you had the decency to be dishonest about it. You did not tell me the truth, in spite of all your theories. I might never have found out. You knew better than to shake my belief in our love. But I trusted your philosophy, and flaunted my lovers before you. I never realized--

HE. Be careful, my dear. You are contradicting yourself!

SHE. I know I am. I don't care. I no longer know what the truth is. I only know that I am filled with remorse for what has happened. Why did it happen? Why did we let it happen? Why didn't you stop me? . . . I want it back!

HE. But, Helen!

SHE. Yes--our old happiness.... Don't you remember, Paul, how beautiful everything was--? (She covers her face with her hands, and then looks up again.) Give it back to me, Paul!

HE. (*torn with conflicting wishes*) Do you really believe, Helen...?

SHE. I know we can be happy again. It was all ours, and we must have it once more, just as it was. (*She holds out her hands*.) Paul! Paul!

HE. (*desperately*) Let me think!

SHE. (scornfully) Oh, your thinking! I know! Think, then--think of all the times I've been cruel to you. Think of my wantonness--my wickedness--not of my poor, tormented attempts at happiness. My lovers, yes! Think hard, and save yourself from any more discomfort. . . . But no--you're in no danger. . . .

HE. What do you mean?

SHE. (*laughing hysterically*) You haven't believed what I've been saying all this while, have you?

HE. Almost.

SHE. Then don't. I've been lying.

HE. Again?

SHE. Again, yes.

HE. I suspected it.

SHE. (*mockingly*) Wise man!

HE. You don't love me, then?

SHE. Why should I? Do you want me to?

HE. I make no demands upon you. You know that.

SHE. You can get along without me?

HE. (*coldly*) Why not?

SHE. Good. Then I'll tell you the truth!

HE. That *would* be interesting!

SHE. I was afraid you *did* want me! And--I was sorry for you, Paul--I thought if you did, I would try to make things up to you, by starting over again--if you wanted to.

HE. So that was it. . . .

SHE. Yes, that was it. And so--

HE. (*harshly*) You needn't say any more. Will you go, or shall I?

SHE. (*lightly*) I'm going, Paul. But I think--since we may not meet this time next year--that I'd better tell you the secret of that third time. When you asked me a while ago, I cried, and said I couldn't talk about it. But I can now.

HE. You mean--

SHE. Yes. My last cruelty. I had a special reason for being cruel to you. Shan't I tell you?

HE. Just as you please.

SHE. My reason was this: I had learned what it is to love--and I knew that I had never loved you--never. I wanted to hurt you so much that you would leave me. I wanted to hurt you in such a way as to keep you from ever coming near me again. I was afraid that if you did forgive me and take me in your arms, you would feel me shudder, and see the terror and loathing in my eyes. I wanted--for even then I cared for you a little--to spare you that.

HE. (*speaking with difficulty*) Are you going?

SHE. (lifting from the table a desk calendar, and tearing a leaf from it, which she holds in front of him. Her voice is tender with an inexplicable regret.) Did you notice the date? It is the eighth of June. Do you remember what day that is? We used to celebrate it once a year. It is the day--(the leaf flutters to the table in front of him)--the day of our first kiss. . . .

He sits looking at her. For a moment it seems clear to him that they still love each other, and that a single word from him, a mere gesture, the holding out of his arms to her, will reunite them. And then he doubts. . . . She is watching him; she turns at last toward the door, hesitates, and then walks slowly out. When she has gone he takes up the torn leaf from the calendar, and holds it in his hands, looking at it with the air of a man confronted by an unsolvable enigma.

IBSEN REVISITED

A PIECE OF FOOLISHNESS

TO LOUIS UNTERMEYER

"Ibsen Revisited" was first produced at the Liberal Club, in 1914, with the following cast:

The Maid .... Jo Gotsch
The Stranger...... Floyd Dell

A middle-class interior. The parlour-maid is dusting the furniture.

THE MAID. Oh, how dull it is here! Nobody to talk to, nobody to flirt with. . . . Flirt! The men that come to this house don't even know the meaning of the word. I never worked in such a place. Life is just one long funeral. I wish something would happen. (*A knock at the door.*) Ah! if it were only in the old days, one might hope that that was a reporter. But nothing like that now!

She opens the door. A stranger enters.

THE STRANGER. Is--ah--Miss Gabler in?

THE MAID. You mean--Mrs. Lovberg?

THE STRANGER. Yes--but . . . I'm not mistaken, am I? Mrs. Lovberg is-- or was--Hedda Gabler. Isn't that true?

THE MAID. Oh, yes, it's Hedda. But she prefers to be called by her husband's name. Did you wish to see her? She is busy just now.

THE STRANGER. Busy?

THE MAID. Yes--she is conducting her class in Modern Adolescence.

THE STRANGER. How like Hedda! Always experimenting with something or other! What is she teaching them?

THE MAID. She's teaching them what she calls "sex-unconsciousness."

THE STRANGER. Dear me! *What* is sex-unconsciousness?

THE MAID. I'm sure *I* don't know, sir.

THE STRANGER. Dear, delightful Hedda! Ever in pursuit of the new sensation!

THE MAID. You are an old friend of hers, I suppose?

THE STRANGER. Well, no, not exactly. The fact is--

THE MAID. You're not a reporter, are you? Hedda doesn't talk to reporters--any more.

THE STRANGER. No. I'm not a reporter.

THE MAID. What are you, then?

THE STRANGER. I am the representative of the International Ibsen Society. You know who Ibsen was, of course?

THE MAID. Yes--he was that nasty man who wrote plays about everybody's private affairs.

THE STRANGER. There *is* that point of view, of course. I'm sorry to intrude--

THE MAID. I should think you would be! Now that she and Lovberg are happily married--

THE STRANGER. That's precisely it. You see, we've just discovered that instead of committing suicide, as Ibsen made them do in the play, they eloped and were eventually married. You can't imagine how delighted we all are to discover that Hedda is still alive. As soon as we found that out, I was sent here immediately--

THE MAID. What did you think you would see?

THE STRANGER. See? I shall see a woman whose soul burns with an unquenchable flame of divine adventurousness. I shall see the most ardent, impatient, eager, restless, impetuous, and insatiably romantic woman in the world.

THE MAID. (*pointing to the door*) You mean--her?

THE STRANGER. Yes--why, there is the very sofa upon which she and Lovberg used to sit, in the old days, discussing his past. There he would sit and tell her of his escapades, his affairs, everything. Tell me, does she insist on Lovberg's being polygamous, whether he wants to or not?

THE MAID. Evidently you don't know the new Hedda. Or the new Lovberg either. The only thing they talk about is what they call "the monogamist ideal."

THE STRANGER. There is some mistake. I will find out when I see her. Surely she is still interested in adventure--the free life--vine-leaves--beauty--! I will remind her of her own past--

THE MAID. No you won't. She won't let you. She will tell you that too much attention is paid to such foolishness nowadays.

THE STRANGER. She! who was interested in nothing else! But then--what is she interested in, now?

THE MAID. In "co-operation."

THE STRANGER, Has she then turned into a mere sociologist? Oh, you are deceiving me!

THE MAID. If you don't believe me--I'll just open the door an inch, and you can hear her talking.

THE STRANGER. Oh, it cannot be true!

The maid quietly opens the door a little way. He listens.

A VOICE. (*heard through the aperture*) We must all learn to function socially. . . .

The maid shuts the door again.

THE MAID. Do you believe it now?

THE STRANGER. (*sadly*) It is too true!

THE MAID. Didn't I tell you?

THE STRANGER. So Hedda has become--a reformer!

THE MAID. Yes.

THE STRANGER. And Lovberg--what does he do?

THE MAID. He is rewriting his book--you know, the one Hedda burned up--for use as a text-book in the public schools. And Hedda is helping him.

THE STRANGER. No more adventure--no more beauty--the flame . . . gone out! My God!

He staggers toward the wall, where a pistol is hanging, and puts his hand on it.

THE MAID. Look out! That's Hedda's pistol. You never can tell when an old piece of junk like that is loaded.

THE STRANGER. Yes--I know. (He takes it down and aims it at his heart.) The old Hedda is gone. I cannot bear the new. It would be too--(*The maid screams*)--too dull.

He fires, and falls.

THE MAID. (*going over and looking down at him*) But--people don't do such things!

KING ARTHUR'S SOCKS

A COMEDY

To MAX EASTMAN

"King Arthur's Socks" was first produced by the Provincetown Players, New York City, in 1916, with the following cast:

Guenevere Robinson...Edna James
Vivien Smith.........Jane Burr
Mary.................Augusta Gary
Lancelot Jones.......Max Eastman

The living room of a summer cottage in Camelot, Maine. A pretty woman of between twenty-five and thirty-five is sitting in a big chair in the lamplight darning socks. She is Mrs. Arthur B. Robinson--or, to give her her own name, Guenevere. She is dressed in a light summer frock, and with her feet elevated on a settle there is revealed a glimpse of slender silk-clad ankles. It is a pleasant summer evening, and, one might wonder why so attractive a woman should be sitting at home darning her husband's socks, there being so many other interesting things to do in this world. The girl standing in the doorway, smiling amusedly, seems to wonder at it too. The girl's name is Vivien Smith.

VIVIEN. Hello, Gwen!

GUENEVERE. Hello, Vivien! Come in.

VIVIEN. I'm just passing by.

GUENEVERE. Come in and console me for a minute or two, anyway. I'm a widow at present.

VIVIEN. (*enters and lounges against the mantelpiece*) Arthur gone to New York again?

GUENEVERE. Yes, for over Sunday. And I'm lonely.

VIVIEN. You don't seem to mind. Think of a woman being that happy darning her husband's socks!

GUENEVERE. Stay here and talk to me--unless you've something else on. It's been ages since I've seen you.

VIVIEN. I'm afraid I have got something else on, Gwen--I'll give you one guess.

GUENEVERE. You can't pretend to be art-ing at this hour of the night.

VIVIEN. I could pretend, but I won't. No, Gwen dear, it's not the pursuit of art, it's the pursuit of a man.

GUENEVERE. Don't try to talk like a woman in a Shaw play. I don't like this rigmarole about "pursuit." Say you're in love, like a civilized human being. And take a cigarette, and tell me about it.

VIVIEN. (lighting a cigarette) I don't know whether I'm so civilized, at that. You know me, Gwen. When I paint, do I paint like a lady?--or like a savage! (She does, in fact, appear to be a very headstrong and reckless young woman.)

GUENEVERE. (*mildly*) Oh, be a savage all you want to, Gwen. But don't tell me you're going in for this modern free-love stuff, because I won't believe it. You're not that kind of fool, Vivien. (She darns placidly away.)

VIVIEN. No, I'm not. I'm not a fool at all, Gwen dear. I know exactly what I want--and it doesn't include being disowned by my family and having my picture in the morning papers. Free-love? Not at all. I want to be married.

GUENEVERE. Well, for heaven's sake, who is it?

VIVIEN. Is it possible that it's not being gossiped about? You really haven't heard?

GUENEVERE. Not a syllable.

VIVIEN. Then I shan't tell you.

GUENEVERE. But--why?

VIVIEN. Because you'll think I've a nerve to want him.

GUENEVERE. Nonsense. I don't know any male person in these parts who is good enough for you, Vivien.

VIVIEN. Thanks, darling. That's just what I think in my calmer moments. But mostly I'm so crazy about him that I'm almost humble. Can you imagine it?

GUENEVERE. Well, what's the matter, then? Doesn't he reciprocate? You don't look like the victim of a hopeless passion.

VIVIEN. Oh, he's in love with me all right. But he doesn't want to be. He says being in love interferes with his work.

GUENEVERE. What nonsense!

VIVIEN. Oh, I don't know about that! I think being in love with me would interfere with a man's work. I should hope so!

GUENEVERE. (*primly*) I don't interfere with Arthur's work.

VIVIEN. Arthur's a professor of philosophy. Besides, Arthur had written a book and settled down before he fell in love with you. I'm dealing with a man who has his work still to do. He thinks if he had about three years of peace and quiet and hard work, he'd put something big across. He put it up to me as a fellow-artist. I know just how he feels. I suppose I am very distracting!

GUENEVERE. Well, why don't you give him his three years?

VIVIEN. Gwen! What do you think I am? An altruist? A benefactor of humanity? Well, I'm not, I'm a woman. Three years? I've given him three hours, and threatened to marry a man back at home if he doesn't make up his mind before then.

GUENEVERE. Heavens, Vivien, you *are* a savage! Well, did it work?

VIVIEN. I don't know. The three hours aren't up yet. I'm going around to get my answer now. I must say the prospect isn't encouraging. He started to pack up to go to Boston. He says he won't be bullied.

GUENEVERE. But Vivien!

VIVIEN. Oh, don't condole with me yet, Gwen dear. It's twelve hours before that morning train, and I'm not through with him yet.

GUENEVERE. (*curiously*) What are you going to do?

VIVIEN. Nothing crude, Gwen dear. Oh, there's lots of things I can do. Cry, for instance. He's never seen a woman cry. Maybe you think I can't cry?

GUENEVERE. It's hard to imagine *you* crying.

VIVIEN. I never wanted anything badly enough to cry for it before. But I could cry my heart out for him. I've absolutely no pride left. Well-- I'm going to have him, that's all. (She throws her cigarette into the grate, and starts to go .)

GUENEVERE. And what about his work? Suppose it's true--

VIVIEN. Suppose it is. Then his work will have to get along the best way it can. (**She turns at the door** .) Do I look like a loser?--or a winner!

GUENEVERE. I'll bet on you, Vivien.

VIVIEN. Thanks, darling. And bye-bye.

GUENEVERE. (*stopping her*) But Vivien--! I've been racking my brain to think who--? **Do** tell me!

VIVIEN. (*in the doorway, defiantly*) Well, if you must know--it's Lancelot Jones.

GUENEVERE. (*springing up, amazed, incredulous and horrified*) Oh, **no**, Vivien! Not Lancelot!

VIVIEN. Absolutely yes.

GUENEVERE. But--but he's married already!

VIVIEN. Oh, is **that** what's bothering you?

GUENEVERE. I should rather think it would bother **you**, Vivien!

VIVIEN. But it so happens that it doesn't. I'm not breaking up a marriage. There isn't any marriage there to break up. I know all about it. Lancelot told me. That marriage was ended long ago. It's simply that he has never got a divorce.

GUENEVERE. But--but if that's true, why **hasn't** he got a divorce?

VIVIEN. On purpose, Gwen--as a protection! Against love-sick females like me. Against getting married again. I told you he wanted to work.

GUENEVERE. But Vivien! If he hasn't got a divorce--

VIVIEN. He'll have to get one, that's all. It won't take long. And in the meantime we can be engaged.

GUENEVERE. A funny sort of engagement, Vivien--to a married man!

VIVIEN. I think you're very unkind, Gwen. It isn't funny at all. It's a nuisance. We'll have to wait at least a month! I think you might sympathize with me. I believe you're in love with him yourself.

GUENEVERE. (*coldly*) Vivien!

VIVIEN. (*contritely*) I'm sorry. I didn't mean it. But I do think he's so terribly nice--I don't see how any woman can help being in love with him. Well--I'm off to his studio, to learn my fate. Wish me luck, if you can!

She goes.

GUENEVERE. (looks after her, then drifts over to the mantel, leans against it staring out into space, and then murmurs)--Lancelot!

She goes slowly back to her chair, sits still a moment, and then quietly resumes the darning of socks.

Enter, from the side door, Mary, the pretty servant girl, who fusses about at the back of the room.

GUENEVERE. (*absently*) Going, Mary?

MARY. No, ma'am. I don't feel like going out tonight.

Something in her tone makes Guenevere turn.

GUENEVERE. (*kindly*) Why, Mary, what is the matter?

MARY. (*struggling with her sobs*) I'm sorry, ma'am, I can't help it--I wasn't going to say anything. But when you spoke to me--

GUENEVERE. (*quietly*) What is it, Mary?

MARY. I'm a wicked girl. (**She sobs again**.)

GUENEVERE. (**after a moment's reflection**.) Yes? Tell me about it.

MARY. Shall I tell you?

GUENEVERE. Yes. I think you'd better tell me.

MARY. I wanted to tell you. (She comes to Guenevere, and sinks beside her chair.) I wanted to tell you before Mr. Robinson came back. I couldn't tell you if he was here.

GUENEVERE. (**smiling**) My husband? Are you afraid of him, Mary?

MARY. Yes, ma'am.

GUENEVERE. (**to herself**) Poor Arthur! He does frighten people. He looks so--just.

MARY. That's what it is, ma'am. He always makes me think of my father.

GUENEVERE. Is your father a just man, too, Mary?

MARY. Yes, ma'am. He's that just I'd never dare breathe a word to him about what I've done. He'd put me out of the house.

GUENEVERE. (**hesitating**) Is it so bad, Mary, what you have done?

MARY. Yes, ma'am.

GUENEVERE. Do you--do you want to tell me who it is?

MARY. It's Mr. Jones, ma'am.

GUENEVERE. (*reflectively*) Jones? (*Then, astoundedly*)--Jones! (*Incredulously*)--You don't mean--! (*Quietly*)--Do you mean Mr. Lancelot Jones?

MARY. Yes, ma'am.

GUENEVERE. This is terrible! When did it happen?

MARY. It--it sort of happened last night, ma'am. It was this way--

GUENEVERE. No details, please!

MARY. No, ma'am. I just wanted to tell you how it was. You see, ma'am, I went to his studio--

GUENEVERE. (*unable to bear it*) Please, Mary, please!

MARY. Yes, ma'am.

GUENEVERE. I don't mean that I blame you. One can't help--falling in love....

MARY. No, you just can't help it, can you?

GUENEVERE. But Lancelot--Mr. Jones--should have behaved better than that....

MARY. Should he, ma'am?

GUENEVERE. He certainly should. I wouldn't have believed it of him. So that is why--Mary! Do you know--? But I'm not sure that I ought to tell you. Still, I don't see why I should protect *him*. Do you know that he is going away?

MARY. No, ma'am. Is he?

GUENEVERE. Yes. In the mo'rning. You must go to see him tonight. No, you can't do that....Oh, this is terrible!

MARY. I'm *glad* he's going away, Mrs. Robinson.

GUENEVERE. Are you?

MARY. Yes, ma'am.

GUENEVERE. Why?

MARY. Because I'd be so ashamed every time I saw him.

GUENEVERE. (*looking at her with interest*) Really? I didn't know people felt that way. Perhaps it's the right way to feel. But I didn't suppose anybody did. So you want him to go?

MARY. Yes, ma'am.

GUENEVERE. And you don't feel you've any claim on him?

MARY. No, ma'am. Why should I?

GUENEVERE. Well! I really don't know. But one is supposed to. Mary, you *are* a modern woman!

MARY. Am I?

GUENEVERE. One would think, after what happened--

MARY. That's just it, ma'am. If it had been anything else--But after what happened, I just want never to see him again. You see, ma'am, it was this way--

GUENEVERE. (*gently*) Is it necessary to tell me that, Mary? I know what happened.

MARY. But you don't, ma'am. That's just it. I've been trying to tell you what happened, ma'am.

GUENEVERE. Good heavens, was it so horrible! Well, go on, then. (She nerves herself to hear the worst.) What *did* happen?

MARY. Nothing, ma'am....

GUENEVERE. Nothing?

MARY. That's just it....

GUENEVERE. But I--I don't understand.

MARY. You said a while ago, Mrs. Robinson, that you couldn't help falling in love. It's true. I tried every way to stop, but I couldn't. So last night I--I went to his studio--

GUENEVERE. Yes?

MARY. I told you I was a wicked girl, Mrs. Robinson. You know I've a key to let myself in to clean up for him. So last night I just went in. He--he was asleep--

GUENEVERE. Yes?

MARY. I--shall I tell you, ma'am?

GUENEVERE. Yes. You *must* tell me, now.

MARY. And I--(She sits kneeling, looking straight ahead, and continues speaking, in a dead voice) I couldn't help it. I put my arms around him.

GUENEVERE. Yes?

MARY. And he put his arms around me, Mrs. Robinson, and kissed me. And I didn't care about anything else, then. I was glad. And then--

GUENEVERE. Yes?

MARY. And then he woke up--and he was angry at me. He swore at me. And then he laughed, and kissed me again, and put me out of the room.

GUENEVERE. Yes, yes. And that--that was all?

MARY. I came home. I thought I would have died. I knew I had been wicked. Oh, Mrs. Robinson--(**She breaks down and sobs**.)

GUENEVERE. (**patting her head**) Poor child, it's all right. You aren't so wicked as you think. Oh, I'm so glad!

MARY. But it's jest the same, Mrs. Robinson. I wanted to be wicked.

GUENEVERE. Never mind, Mary. We all want to be wicked at times. But something always happens. It's all right. You're a good girl, Mary. There, stop crying!... Of course, of course! I might have known.

Lancelot couldn't--and yet, I wonder.... Mary, stand up and let me look at you!

MARY. (*obeying*) Yes, ma'am.

GUENEVERE. (*in a strange tone*) You're a very good-looking girl, Mary.... So he laughed, and gave you a kiss, and led you to the door!... Well! Go to bed and think no more about it. It's all right.

MARY. Do you really think so, Mrs. Robinson? Isn't it the same thing if you *want* to be wicked--

GUENEVERE. You're talking like a professor of philosophy now, Mary. And you're a woman, and you ought to know better. No, it isn't the same thing, at all. Run along, child.

MARY. Yes, ma'am. Thank you, ma'am. Good night, ma'am.

She goes.

GUENEVERE. Good-night, Mary. (She returns to her darning. She smiles to herself, then becomes serious, stops work, and looks at the clock. Then she says)--Vivien! Vivien's tears! Poor Lancelot! Oh, well! (She shrugs her shoulders, and goes on working. Then suddenly she puts down her work, rises, and walks restlessly about the room.... There is a knock at the door. She turns and stares at the door. The knock is repeated. She is silent, motionless for a moment. Then she says, almost in a whisper)--Come!

A young man enters.

GUENEVERE. Lancelot!

LANCELOT. Guenevere! (They go up to each other, and he takes both her hands. They stand that way for a moment. Then he says lightly) --Darning King Arthur's socks, I see!

GUENEVERE. (*releasing herself, and going back to her chair*) Yes. Sit down.

LANCELOT. Where's his royal highness?

GUENEVERE. New York. Why don't you ever come to see us?

LANCELOT. (*not answering*) Charming domestic picture!

GUENEVERE. Don't be silly!

LANCELOT. I am going away.

GUENEVERE. Are you? I'm sorry. Don't you like our little village?

LANCELOT. Thought I'd stop in to say good-bye.

GUENEVERE. That's very sweet of you.

LANCELOT. (*rising*) I've got to go back and finish packing.

GUENEVERE. Not really?

LANCELOT. Going in the morning.

GUENEVERE. Why the haste? The summer's just begun. I hear you've been doing some awfully good things. I was going over to see them.

LANCELOT. Thanks. Sorry to disappoint you. But I've taken it into my head to leave.

GUENEVERE. You're not going tonight, anyway. Sit down and talk to me.

LANCELOT. All right. (*He sits, constrainedly*.) What shall I talk about?

GUENEVERE. (*smiling*) Your work.

LANCELOT. (*impatiently*) You're not interested in my work.

GUENEVERE. Your love-affairs, then.

LANCELOT. Don't want to.

GUENEVERE. Then read to me. There's some books on the table.

LANCELOT. (*opening a serious-looking magazine*) Here's an article on "The Concept of Happiness"--by Professor Arthur B. Robinson. Shall I read that?

GUENEVERE. I gather that you are not as fond of my husband as I am, Lancelot. But try to be nice to me, anyway. Read some poetry.

LANCELOT. (*takes a book from the table, and reads*)--

"It needs no maxims drawn from Socrates
  To tell me this is madness in my blood--"

He pauses. She looks up inquiringly. Presently he goes on reading--

"Nor does what wisdom I have learned from these
  Serve to abate my most unreasoned mood.

What would I of you? What gift could you bring,
That to await you in the common street
Sets all my secret ecstasy a-wing
Into wild regions of sublime retreat?
And if you come, you will speak common words--"

He stops, and flings the book across the room. She looks up.

GUENEVERE. Don't you like it?

LANCELOT. (*gloomily*) Hell! That's too true.

GUENEVERE. Try something else.

LANCELOT. No--I can't read. (*Guenevere bends to her darning*.)
Shall I go?

GUENEVERE. No.

LANCELOT. Do you enjoy seeing me suffer?

GUENEVERE. Does talking to me make you suffer?

LANCELOT. Yes.

GUENEVERE. I'm sorry.

LANCELOT. Then let me go.

GUENEVERE. No. Sit there and talk to me, like a rational human being.

LANCELOT. I'm not a rational human being. I'm a fool. A crazy fool.

GUENEVERE. (*smiling at him*) I like crazy fools.

LANCELOT. (*desperately, rising as he speaks*) I am going to be married.

GUENEVERE. (*in a mocking simulation of surprise*) What, again?

LANCELOT. Yes--again--and as soon as possible--to Vivien.

GUENEVERE. I congratulate you.

LANCELOT. I *love* her.

GUENEVERE. Naturally.

LANCELOT. *She* loves *me*.

GUENEVERE. I trust so.

LANCELOT. Then *why* should I be at this moment aching to kiss *you*? Tell me that?

GUENEVERE. (*looking at him calmly*) It does seem strange.

LANCELOT. It is absolutely insane! It's preposterous! It's contradictory!

GUENEVERE. Are you quite sure it's all true?

LANCELOT. Yes! I'm sure that I never would commit the rashness of matrimony again without being in love. Very much in love. And I'm equally sure that I would not stand here and tell you what a fool I am about you, if *that* weren't true. Do you think I *want* to be this

way? It's too ridiculous--I didn't want to tell you. I wanted to go.
You made me stay. Well, now you know what a blithering lunatic I am.

GUENEVERE. (*quietly*) It **is** lunacy, isn't it?

LANCELOT. Is it?

GUENEVERE. Sheer lunacy. In love with one woman, and wanting to kiss
another. Disgraceful, in fact.

LANCELOT. I know what you think! You think I'm paying you an extremely
caddish compliment--or else--

GUENEVERE. (**earnestly, as she rises**) No, I don't think that at
all, Lancelot. I believe you when you say that about me. And I don't
imagine for one moment that you're not really in love with Vivien. I
know you are. I could pretend to myself that you weren't--just as
you've tried to pretend to yourself sometimes, that I'm not really in
love with Arthur. But you know I am--don't you?

LANCELOT. Yes. ...

GUENEVERE. Well, Lancelot, there are--two lunatics here. (He stares
at her.) It's almost funny. I don't know why I'm telling you. But--

LANCELOT. You--!

GUENEVERE. Yes. I want to kiss you, too.

LANCELOT. But this won't do. As long as there was only one of us--

GUENEVERE. There's been two all along, Lancelot. I've more self-control
than you--that's all. But I broke down tonight. I knew I oughtn't to

tell you--now. But I knew I would.

LANCELOT. You, too!

They have unconsciously circled about to the opposite side of the room.

GUENEVERE. Oh, well, Lance, I fancy we aren't the only ones. It's a common human failing, no doubt. Lots of people must feel this way.

LANCELOT. What do they do about it?

GUENEVERE. Well, it all depends on what kind of people they are. Some of them go ahead and kiss. Others think of the consequences.

LANCELOT. Well, let's think of the consequences, then. What are they? I forget.

GUENEVERE. I don't. I'm keeping them very clearly in mind. In the first place--

LANCELOT. Yes?

GUENEVERE. What was it? Yes--in the first place, we would be sorry. And in the second place--

LANCELOT. In the second place--

GUENEVERE. In the second place--I forget what's in the second place. But in the third place we mustn't. Isn't that enough?

LANCELOT. Yes. I know we mustn't. But--I feel that we are going to.

GUENEVERE. Please don't say that.

LANCELOT. But isn't it true? Don't you feel that, too?

GUENEVERE. Yes.

LANCELOT. Then we're lost.

GUENEVERE. No. We must think!

LANCELOT. I can't think.

GUENEVERE. Try.

LANCELOT. It's no use. I can't even remember "in the first place," now.

GUENEVERE. Then--before we do remember--!

He takes her in his arms. They kiss each other--a long, long kiss.

LANCELOT. Sweetheart!

GUENEVERE. (*holding him at arm's length*) That was in the second place, Lancelot. If we kiss each other, we'll begin saying things like that--and perhaps believing them.

LANCELOT. What did I say?

GUENEVERE. Something very foolish.

LANCELOT. What, darling?

GUENEVERE. There, you did it again. Stop, or I shall be doing it, too.

I want to, you know.

LANCELOT. Want what?

GUENEVERE. To call you darling, and believe I'm in love with you.

LANCELOT. Aren't you?

GUENEVERE. I mustn't be.

LANCELOT. But aren't you?

GUENEVERE. Oh, I--(She closes her eyes, and he draws her to him. Suddenly she frees herself.) No! Lancelot--no! I'm not in love with you. And you're not in love with me. We're just two wicked people who want to kiss each other.

LANCELOT. Wicked? I don't feel wicked. Do you?

GUENEVERE. No. I just feel natural. But it's the same thing. (He approaches her with outstretched arms. She retreats behind the chair.) No, no. Remember that I'm married.

LANCELOT. I don't care.

GUENEVERE. Then remember that you're engaged!

LANCELOT. Engaged?

GUENEVERE. Yes: to Vivien.

LANCELOT. (*stopping short*) So I am.

GUENEVERE. And you're in love with her.

LANCELOT. That's true.

GUENEVERE. You see now that you can't kiss me, don't you?

LANCELOT (*dazedly*) Yes.

GUENEVERE. Then thank heavens! for I was about to let you. And that's in the fifth place, Lancelot: if we kiss each other once, we're sure to do it again and again--and again. Now go over there and sit down, and we'll talk sanely and sensibly.

LANCELOT. (*obeying*) Heavens, what a moment! I'm not over it yet.

GUENEVERE. Neither am I. We're a pair of sillies, aren't we? I never thought I should ever behave in such a fashion.

LANCELOT. It was my fault. I shouldn't have started it.

GUENEVERE. I am as much to blame as you.

LANCELOT. I'm sorry.

GUENEVERE. Are you?

LANCELOT. I ought to be. But I'm not, exactly.

GUENEVERE. I'm not either, I'm ashamed to say.

LANCELOT. The truth is, I want to kiss you again.

GUENEVERE. And I... But do you call this talking sensibly?

LANCELOT. I suppose it isn't. Well, go ahead with your sixth place, then. Only, for heaven's sake try and say something that will really do some good!

GUENEVERE. Very well, Lancelot. Do you really want to elope with me?

LANCELOT. Very much.

GUENEVERE. That's not the right answer. You know perfectly well you want to do nothing of the sort. What! Scandalize everybody, and ruin my reputation, and break Vivien's heart?

LANCELOT. No--I don't suppose I really want to do any of those things.

GUENEVERE. Then do you want us to conduct a secret and vulgar intrigue?

LANCELOT. (*hurt*) Guenevere!

GUENEVERE. You realize, of course, that this madness of ours might last no longer than a month?

LANCELOT. (*soberly*) Perhaps.

GUENEVERE. Well, do you still want to kiss me?--Think what you are saying, Lancelot, for I may let you. And that kiss may be the beginning of the catastrophe. (*She moves toward him*.) Do you want a kiss that brings with it grief and fear and danger and heartbreak?

LANCELOT. No--

GUENEVERE. Then what do you want?

LANCELOT. I want--a kiss.

GUENEVERE. Never. If you had believed, for one your chance.

LANCELOT. Kiss me!

GUENEVERE. Never. If you had believed, for one moment, that it *was* worth the price of grief and heartbreak, I should have believed it too, and kissed you, and not cared what happened. I should have risked the love of my husband and the happiness of your sweetheart without a qualm. And who knows? It might have been worth it. An hour from now I shall be sure it wasn't; I shall be sure it was all blind, wicked folly. But now I am a little sorry. I wanted to gamble with fate. I wanted us to stake our two lives recklessly upon a kiss--and see what happened. And you couldn't. It wasn't a moment of beauty and terror to you. You didn't want to challenge fate. You just wanted to kiss me.... Go!

LANCELOT. (*turning on her bitterly*) You women! Because you are afraid, you accuse us of being cowards.

GUENEVERE. What do you mean?

LANCELOT. (*brutally*) You! You want a love-affair. Your common sense tells you it's folly. Your reason won't allow it. So you want your common sense to be overwhelmed, your reason lost. You want to be swept off your, feet. You want to be *made* to do something you don't approve of. You want to be wicked, and you want it to be some one else's fault. Tell me--isn't it true?

GUENEVERE. Yes, it is true--except for one thing, Lancelot. It's true that I wanted you to sweep me off my feet, to make me forget everything; it was wrong, it was foolish of me to want it, but I did. Only if you had done it, you wouldn't have been "to blame." I should have loved you for ever because you could do it. And now, because you couldn't I despise you. Now you know. ... Go.

LANCELOT. No, Guenevere, you don't despise me. You're angry with me and angry with yourself because you couldn't quite forget King Arthur. You are blaming me and I am blaming you, isn't it amusing?

GUENEVERE. You are right, Lancelot. It's my fault. Oh, I envy women who can dare to make fools of themselves who forget everything and don't care what they do! I suppose that's love--and I'm not up to it.

LANCELOT. You are different....

GUENEVERE. Different? Yes, I'm a coward. I'm not primitive enough. Despise me. You've a right to. And--please go.

LANCELOT. I'm afraid I'm not very primitive either, Gwen. I--

GUENEVERE. I'm afraid you're not, Lance. That's the trouble with us. We're civilized. Hopelessly civilized. We had a spark of the old barbaric flame--but it went out. We put it out--quenched it with conversation. No, Lancelot, we've talked our hour away. It's time for you to pack up. Good-bye. (*He kisses her hand lingeringly*.) You may kiss my lips if you like. There's not the slightest danger. We were unnecessarily alarmed about ourselves. We couldn't misbehave! ... Going?

LANCELOT. Damn you! Good-bye!

He goes.

GUENEVERE. Well, *that* did it. If he had stayed a moment longer--!

She flings up her arms in a wild gesture--then recovers herself, and goes to her chair, where she sits down and quietly resumes the darning of her husband's socks.

THE RIM OF THE WORLD

A FANTASY

To MARJORIE JONES

"The Rim of the World" was first produced by the Liberal Club, New York City, at Webster Hall, in 1915, with the following cast:

The Maid .... Jo Gotsch
The Gypsy .... Floyd Dell
The King.......... Edward Goodman
The Princess...... Marjorie Jones

Morning. A room in a palace, opening on a balcony. Through the arched broad window at the back is seen the sky, just beginning to be suffused with the rosy streakings of dawn. A large, wide heavy seat stands on a dais, with a low square stool beside it. A girl kneels on the stool, with her head and arms on the chair, dozing.

The dark figure of a man appears on the balcony. He puts a leg over the window-ledge and climbs in slowly.

A little noise wakes the girl. She stirs, looks round, jumps up, and starts to scream .

THE MAN. Oh, not so loud!

THE GIRL. (*finishes the scream in a subdued voice*.)

THE MAN. That's better! But you ought to be more careful. You might wake somebody up.

THE GIRL. Who are you?

THE MAN. That's just what I was about to ask you--tell me, are you a Princess, or a maidservant?

THE GIRL. A Princess?--did you really think I might be a Princess?

THE MAN. Well, there are pretty Princesses. But I had rather you were a maidservant.

THE GIRL. Would you? Well, so I am!

THE MAN. Thank you, my dear. And what would you like me to be?

THE MAID. I'm afraid you're somebody not quite proper!

THE MAN. Right, my dear. You are a person of marvellous discernment. I am, in fact--

THE MAID. The king of the Gypsies!

THE GYPSY. How did you know?

THE GIRL. I guessed it!

THE GYPSY. H'm. You knew, I suppose, that our band has just encamped outside the city?

THE MAID. Yes.

THE GYPSY. And you have heard of the exploits of the Gypsy king. You know that there is no wall high enough to keep him out, no force of soldiers strong enough--

THE MAID. I know it by your eyes. They have the gypsy look in them.

THE GYPSY. Where have you ever seen gypsies before?

THE MAID. Never mind. But tell me--the wall around the palace is seventeen feet high--

THE GYPSY. True enough!

THE MAID. A guard of soldiers continually marches around it--

THE GYPSY. Very true!

THE MAID. And there are spikes on the top. How did you get over?

THE GYPSY. That is my secret. Would I be the gypsy king if everybody knew what I know?

THE MAID. Won't you tell *me*?

THE GYPSY. Women have asked me that many times. But I never tell. But, though I won't tell you how I entered, I don't mind telling you *why*.

THE MAID. Oh, I know that already!

THE GYPSY. You think, perhaps, that I am a thief as well as a housebreaker--that it is in the hope of royal treasure left unguarded that I have come here. ...

THE MAID. You have come here because you took a fancy to see what was on the other side of the wall. Isn't that it?

THE GYPSY. At last I have found some one in this stupid city who understands me. Young woman--

THE MAID. Yes?

THE GYPSY. You do not belong here. There is no one here who does things because they are foolish and interesting. Would you like to come away with me?

THE MAID. Oh, no. You must not think, because I understand you, that I approve of you. You see--

THE GYPSY. You don't approve of me?

THE MAID. No--but I like you. I can't help it. I always did like Gypsies. You see, I was brought up among them.

THE GYPSY. You a Gypsy child!

THE MAID. I suppose I was. Though I always preferred to imagine that I was some Princess that had been changed in the cradle and stolen away. When I was hardly more than a baby, I remember that I disapproved of their rough ways. I can still faintly remember the jolting of the wagons that kept me awake, and the smell of the soup in the big kettle over the fire.

THE GYPSY. It is a good smell.

THE MAID. But I did not think so! It smelled of garlic. And when I was six years old, I ran away. The tribe had encamped just outside the city here, and I wandered away from the tents, and entered the city-gate, and hid myself, and at night I came straight to the palace. The soldiers found me, and took me to the old king. He said that I should be the child of the palace. So they gave me white bread with butter on it, and put me to sleep between smooth white sheets.

THE GYPSY. Gypsy children cannot thrive when they are taken into cities. They turn away from white bread with butter on it, and remembering the good smell of the soup in the big kettle over the fire, they fall sick with hunger. As for you--

THE MAID. I thrived on the white bread with butter on it.

THE GYPSY. You were a little renegade. But I forgive you! And now to my business, I have come to see the King, and talk with him. We kings should become better acquainted, don't you think? I will ask him what he considers the proper price for telling fortunes, and find out what his ideas are on the subject of horse-trading. And no doubt he will ask me what I think about his coming marriage with the Princess of Basque. She is to arrive to-night, I believe, and be married tomorrow, to this King whom she has never seen!

THE MAID. Be careful, or you will awaken him. That is his bed-chamber, there.

THE GYPSY. Ah! Is he a light sleeper?

THE MAID. The King sleeps soundly, and awakens punctually every morning at six.

THE GYPSY. (*with a glance at the sky*) It is not quite six. Every morning, you say? And what then?

THE MAID. He goes for a walk at seven, and breakfasts at eight. Every morning.

THE GYPSY. Regularly?

THE MAID. The King is always on time to the moment.

THE GYPSY. Ah, one of those clockwork kings!

THE MAID. You must not make fun of him. He is a good king.

THE GYPSY. I have no doubt of it. And his regularity will be a great comfort to his queen. She will always know that she will get her kiss regularly, punctually, on the stroke of the clock. But--you say the King rises at six, and goes for a walk at seven. What does he do in the meantime?

THE MAID. First he comes here and has his morning drink. Then he is dressed for his walk.

THE GYPSY. And what is your part in these solemn proceedings?

THE MAID. I tie his slippers for him, and pour his drink.

THE GYPSY. It is a great honour! So great an honour that you come here before the sun is up to be ready for your duties. Do you entertain the King with conversation while he takes his morning drink?

THE MAID. No--the Gazetteer does that.

THE GYPSY. The Gazetteer--what is the Gazetteer?

THE MAID. The Gazetteer is a man whose duty it is to find out all that happens in the city each day, and recite it to the King the next morning.

THE GYPSY. Has the King as much curiosity as that? I would never have thought it.

THE MAID. It isn't curiosity. It's just a custom that has sprung up. All the merchants and well-to-do people hire a Gazetteer. It may be useful to them--but I think the King regards it more as a duty than a pleasure.

THE GYPSY. I remember now. They have something like it in the taverns. I foresee a great future for it....

THE MAID. And it seems to go with that new drink.

THE GYPSY. What new drink?

THE MAID. Why, the new drink from Arabia. It has a queer name. Ka-Fe.

THE GYPSY. Ka-Fe--and what is it like?

THE MAID. It is dark, and served hot with sugar and cream.

THE GYPSY. It sounds interesting. I would like to taste it. What is it most like--mead, perhaps, or wine, or that strong liquor distilled from juniper berries?

THE MAID. Like none of these. It does not make men talk and sing and tell their secrets and reveal their love and their hate, and knock their heads against the stars and tangle their feet one with the other....

THE GYPSY. Then what is the good of it?

THE MAID. It makes the head clearer, and sobers the judgment. It makes men think more and talk less. And it gives them strength to rule their inward feelings.

THE GYPSY. What a pity! People are too much like that as it is.

THE MAID. The King says that some time the whole world will learn to drink it!

THE GYPSY. A world of Ka-Fe drinkers! A world where people rule their inward feelings and hide their secret thoughts! I shall be dead before then, thank heaven!

THE MAID. But you keep your secrets--even from women--so you say.

THE GYPSY. It was a vain boast. Sometime, with my head in a woman's lap, I shall blab away the secrets that give me power. I know it. Somewhere in the world is a woman whose look will intoxicate me more than wine. And for her sake I shall invent some new folly.

THE MAID. What a pity!

THE GYPSY. No--the thought cheers me. So long as there are women, men will be fools. Their Ka-Fe will not help them.

THE MAID. Do you approve of folly, then?

THE GYPSY. It is the thing that makes life worth living. I have committed every kind of folly I know, and the world would be dull and empty if I did not think that some new and greater folly lay ahead.

THE MAID. You think, then, that one should surrender oneself to folly?

THE GYPSY. I think so truly. What have you on the tip of your tongue? What folly have you given yourself to, my child?

THE MAID. I am afraid you will laugh at me. ...

THE GYPSY. Not I. Tell me, my dear, are you in love?

THE MAID. Yes....

THE GYPSY. With some one who will never give you love in return?

THE MAID. Yes. ...

THE GYPSY. And is it--?

THE MAID. The King--yes. Oh, I am a fool to tell you!

She hides her face in her hands.

THE GYPSY. Listen, my child. You are not more a fool than I. The other day I rode out on a swift horse to be by myself under the sky, and think my thoughts. And there, a two days' journey from this city, I saw the slow-moving caravan of the Princess of Basque, on her way to wed this King whom she has never seen. Curiosity drew me near, for I wanted to see the face of the Princess. I tied my horse to a tree, and hid among the bushes by the road-side as they passed. I saw her among the cushions of the royal wagon. She had a strange, wild beauty. I saw her, and loved her, and grew sick with loneliness. I rode back to the city, and tried to wash out the memory of that face with wine. But it was no use, so I left the tavern and climbed the wall and entered the palace, that I might look also at the man whom she is to wed. When I have seen him, then I shall--I don't know what. But--we are two foolish ones, you and I!

THE MAID. Thank you for telling me that. But you must go now. It is almost time for the King to come.

THE GYPSY. What if he found me here--what would he do? Have me beheaded, or merely thrown into prison?

THE MAID. No--he is a kind king. He would only tell you how wrong it is to break into people's houses and show disrespect for the law.

THE GYPSY. I had almost rather be put in prison than lectured at. Well, I must invent something to explain my presence. (*There is a knock*.) Who is that?

THE MAID. Hide yourself. I will see.

THE GYSPY. (*from behind the curtains of the window*) I am hidden.

The maid goes to the door, and comes back with a paper in her hand.

THE GYPSY. Well?

THE MAID. (*looking at the paper*) The Gazetteer is ill, and cannot come.

THE GYPSY. (*emerging from the curtains*) The Gazetteer is ill....

THE MAID. The King will be annoyed.

THE GYPSY. We will spare his majesty that annoyance. I shall be the King's Gazetteer this morning!

THE MAID. But how can you?

THE GYPSY. Leave that to me. (He takes his position behind the curtains.) Such news as he has never heard, I shall recite to the King!

THE MAID. Ssh! Here he comes now!

The King enters, in his dressing gown, yawning, with his hand over his mouth. In the midst of his yawn, he speaks.

THE KING. Goo' mo'ing!

THE MAID. (*bowing*) Good morning, your majesty!

THE KING. (*glancing out at the morning sky*) Looks like a nice day today. (*He sits down*.)

THE GYPSY. (*from slightly behind the King's seat*) Not a cloud in your majesty's sky!

THE KING. (*twisting about to look at him*) And who the devil are you?

THE GYPSY. (*coming around in front and bowing*) I am the Gazetteer.

THE KING. (*sputtering*) What are you trying to palm off on me? You are not my Gazetteer! My Gazetteer is decently dressed in black and white. You come here in red and yellow. What does it mean?

THE MAID. Your majesty, your own Gazetteer is ill and cannot come, so he has sent his cousin, who is in the same business.

THE KING. (*disgustedly*) Bring me my Ka-Fe. (*The maid goes out*.) Now tell me, sirrah, you don't mean to say that you are used by respectable people as a source of information? I cannot believe it!

THE GYPSY. Your majesty, it would ill become me to deprecate the character of my clientele. They may not be rich, they may not be influential, but they are the foundation of your kingdom's prosperity. And I must say for myself that for the one person that your Gazetteer serves, I serve many. You may sneer at my quality if you like, but I point to my circulation. I am the official Gazetteer of the Red-Horse Tavern, and scores of petty tradesmen, as well as clerks, bricklayers and truck drivers, depend upon me for their knowledge of the world's events.

THE KING. Well, well! So you are in your humble way an agency of civilization!

THE GYPSY. Your majesty may well say so!

 The maid has returned with the Ka-Fe. She puts the tray on the floor beside the seat, and kneels by it. The King's cup she places on the stool at his hand.

THE KING. (*sipping his Ka-Fe*) Very well. Proceed.

THE GYPSY. (*reciting*) This is the story of a crime! The shop of the widow Solomon stands in the middle of the great street which takes its name from our King--may he live long and prosper! In that shop are displayed for sale diamonds, rubies, emeralds, pearls, and all manner of precious stones, set in rings and chains curiously wrought of silver and gold. And there yesterday came a band of robbers--not in the night, when all men are asleep, and even the watch-dog dozes beside the door-- but in the glare of day, intent on wickedness. They entered the shop, and with the threat of death stopped up the mouths of the servitors. Then they filled a large sack with their precious booty, and escaped. They have not been apprehended. This is the sixth in the series of daring daylight robberies that has occurred within the month. The failure of the police to deal with this situation has provoked widespread comment on the incompetency of the King's Chief of Police, and there are some who assert that the police are in league with the robbers. The magnificent new house which the Chief of Police has been erecting, ostensibly with the money left him by a rich aunt of whom nobody ever heard, seems to lend colour to these--

THE KING. What! What! What's this? Why, I never heard such impudence! Fellow, do you mean to tell me--

He becomes speechless, and sets down his Ka-Fe.

THE GYPSY. Your majesty, I have especially softened the wording of this piece of news in order not to offend your majesty's ears. But in substance that is the story which was told last night at every tavern in the city.

THE KING. But, sirrah, I cannot permit--I simply cannot permit--why-- why--!

THE GYPSY. Suppose, your majesty, we skip the police news, and go on to gentler themes.

THE KING. That would be better--much better.

THE GYPSY. Shall we take up--politics?

THE KING. (*wearily*) Oh, yes.

THE GYPSY. (*reciting*) A debate between the rival factions who seek to influence the governing of our kingdom through the so-called Council of Peers was held last night outdoors in the public market. The rival orators exceeded one another in dullness and hoarseness. The attendance was very slight. The general public takes little interest in these proceedings, knowing as it does that they are merely a diversion for the scions of old families whose energies are unemployed except in time of war. It is the general feeling, moreover, that the King may be depended upon to govern the kingdom properly without the interference of these aristocratic meddlers.

THE KING. Ah, splendid, splendid! Let us hear that again!

THE GYPSY. A debate between the rival factions--

THE KING. No, no--the last part. That about meddling.

THE GYPSY. It is the general feeling, moreover, that the King may be depended upon to govern the kingdom properly--

THE KING. Without interference from these aristocratic meddlers. Yes, yes! Those are my sentiments exactly. How well put that is--without interference! Ah, it shows that I am appreciated among the lower classes. They understand me. What did you say they were? Petty tradesmen and clerks and bricklayers?

THE GYPSY. And truck drivers, your majesty.

THE KING. And truck drivers. Splendid fellows, all of them. As you said--the backbone of my king-dom. I must appoint a royal commission to investigate the welfare of the truck drivers. The Council of Peers will object--but I shall ignore them. Broken-down aristocrats! what do they know about governing a kingdom? They are useful only in war-time. Fighting is their only talent. In times of peace they are a nuisance. I shall not let them come between me and my people. ... (He rises, and with a dignified oratorical gesture addresses an imaginary audience)--Tradesmen! Clerks! Truck drivers! The time has come-- (*He pauses, frowns, and sits down again*.) Never mind that now. Go on with the news.

THE GYSPY. The rest of the political news is uninteresting, your majesty.

THE KING. It usually is. This is the first time it has ever been otherwise. Turn to something else.

THE GYPSY. I will turn to the society items, your majesty.

THE KING. Good.

THE GYPSY. (*reciting*) All tongues are discussing the approaching nuptials of the King and the Princess of--

THE KING. Tut! tut! I fear this is not a proper topic for--

THE GYPSY. It is a matter of interest to all your subjects, your majesty.

THE KING. Well, well--go on. A public figure like myself must submit to having his private affairs discussed. It is unfortunate, but--go on.

THE GYPSY. (*reciting*)--the approaching nuptials of the King and the Princess of Basque. The details of the royal bride's trousseau are already well known to the public, down to the last garter. The six embroidered chemises from Astrakhan--

The maid shows great interest. The King is embarrassed.

THE KING. But, my dear fellow--really, you know--! This is--!

THE GYPSY. Items of this nature, your majesty, are recited in the bazaar to audiences composed exclusively of women. Under the circumstances there is surely no impropriety--

THE KING. Very well. I accept your explanation. But as your present audience is not composed exclusively of women, I suggest that you omit those details.

THE GYPSY. Your majesty, I omit them. The account continues....
(*Reciting*) The marriage has excellent reasons of state for being made, inasmuch as it cements in friendship two kingdoms which have been at war with each other off and on for a hundred years. But it has its romantic side as well. It is, in fact, a love-match. The fact that the royal lovers have never seen each other only emphasizes its romantic quality. Their joy in beholding in actuality what they have for three long months cherished so dearly in imagination, is a theme for the poet laureate--who will, however, we fear, judging from his past performances, hardly do it justice. It is, as we have said, a love-match. The royal pair fell in love with what they had heard of each other--the Princess of Basque with the image she had formed in her mind from glowing reports of the King's valour, amounting to rashness, his fluency of poetic speech, his manly bearing, and his irrepressible wit.... (*The King nods gravely at each item*.) While the King became madly enamoured of the reputation of the Princess of Basque for sweetness, industry in good works, and the docility which befits a wife, even of a King.... (The King nods gravely at these items also.) She is, indeed, a pattern of all the domestic virtues--she

is quiet, obedient, dignified--

There is a cry in a high feminine voice, outside. All look toward
the window. A girl appears, running past, with short loose hair tossing
about her face. She pauses, and flings herself over the window-ledge,
and is standing--panting, red-cheeked, smiling--in the room. The King
rises.

THE KING. (*furious, yet coldly polite*) And who, in the name of
the sacred traditions of womanhood, are you?

THE FIGURE. I--I am the Princess of Basque!

They stare at her.

* * * * *

Mid-day. Yellow curtains have been drawn across the broad window. On
the wide seat, the King, dressed in purple robes, sits with head bowed
in thought.... There is a noise of shouting outside. The King looks
up.

THE KING. (*sadly*) There it is again.

THE GYPSY. (*entering*) Your majesty--

THE KING. You? What are you doing here?

THE GYPSY. Your majesty, the palace is in a turmoil. The attendants are
helping the soldiers keep order among the crowd in the courtyard--the
gentlemen-in-waiting are receiving deputations with wedding presents--
the women are distributing medals bearing the image of the bride. All
the city is celebrating her unexpected arrival, and rejoicing with you

in your presumed happiness. In this disturbed state of affairs, *I* have been drafted into your majesty's service, and come to bring you a message.

THE KING. (*bitterly*) I hoped I would never see you again. It all began with you. If I were a superstitious person I would say you brought misfortune with you into this house. Before you came this morning, everything was as it had always been--orderly and regular. What is your message? That madwoman has not escaped, has she?

THE GYPSY. The young woman who calls herself the Princess of Basque is safe under lock and key, according to your majesty's orders.

THE KING. Is she well guarded?

THE GYPSY. The soldier who conducted her from the room this morning is keeping guard at the door, your majesty. I recognized him by the black eye she gave him.

THE KING. Good. What is your news?

THE GYPSY. Your majesty, I am bidden to tell you that the Royal Archivist, whom you bade to search through the histories of your royal ancestors for some precedent to guide you in this matter, has locked himself with his forty assistants in the royal library, and cannot be roused by knocking.

THE KING. They have fallen asleep among the archives.... What else?

THE GYPSY. Your majesty, the Royal Physician has been summoned, according to your orders, to examine the young woman as to her sanity. But she refuses to answer all questions, asserting that she is in a state of abounding health, and is in no need of the services of a physician.

THE KING. How can we prove her mad if she will not answer questions!

THE GYPSY. Further, I am bidden to tell you that the watchman on the tower has seen two horsemen in the far distance galloping toward the city. They come by the eastern road, and it is believed that they are couriers from the King of Basque.

THE KING. This matter must be settled before they arrive. Is there anything else?

THE GYPSY. Yes, your majesty. The Eldest of the Wise Men has come here in answer to your summons.

THE KING. Bring him in. And do you remain here in attendance.

THE GYPSY. Yes, your majesty.

He goes to the door.

THE KING. This would never have happened to my ancestors. Not to Otho, nor Magnus, nor Carolus, nor Gavaine. Am I less than these? Perhaps I am, but the same blood flows in my veins, and while it flows I shall rule as they ruled.

The Gypsy ushers in the Eldest of the Wise Men.

THE WISE MAN. Your majesty--

THE KING. I have sent for you, O Eldest of the Wise Men, in an hour of extreme perplexity. Not lightly would I have torn you from your meditations. I have need of your wisdom.

THE WISE MAN. Whatever your majesty wishes to know, I shall answer out of the fulness of knowledge born of long study and deep reflection. Speak, O King! Is it of Infinity that you would ask? or of Eternity?-- or of the Absolute?

THE KING. Nothing so simple. I want to know what to do with a madwoman who climbed in at my window an hour since, asserting herself to be the daughter of the King of Basque, and my affianced bride--and with a misguided populace which insists upon celebrating my alleged happiness. (The tumult is heard outside, this time with a harsh note in it. The King starts, turning to the Gypsy.) Is *that* a sound of rejoicing?

THE GYPSY. No, your majesty. That sound means that the rumour has just spread among them that the Princess of Basque has been falsely imprisoned in the palace. They are calling for blood.

THE KING. What! An uprising against me?

THE GYPSY. Not at all, your majesty. They hold your majesty blameless. They believe that you have been deceived by the false counsel of the Eldest of the Wise Men. It is his blood they are calling for.

THE KING. (*to the Eldest of the Wise Men*) There you have it! That, as some one has admirably phrased it, is the situation in a nutshell. What shall we do?

THE WISE MAN. (*stupefied*) But your majesty--!

THE KING. Your advice--what is it? Come, be quick. Out of your wisdom, born of long study and deep reflection, speak the word that shall set this jangled chaos in order once more.

THE WISE MAN. Your majesty, I am afraid I do not understand these things. If you had asked me about the Absolute--

THE KING. There is no Absolute any more! The Absolute has been missing from this kingdom--and for all I know, from the Universe--since half-past six o'clock this morning. No one regrets its absence more than I. There can be no comfort, no peace, no order, without an Absolute. But we must face the facts. The Absolute is gone, and this kingdom will be without one until I restore it with my own hands. I shall set about doing so immediately. And meanwhile, old man, you had better seek some safe corner where my misguided populace cannot lay hands on you.

THE WISE MAN. Your majesty--

THE KING. Go. We have business to attend to. (The Eldest of the Wise Men goes out.) And now, you sharp-nosed scoundrel, I want some of *your* advice! When the roof of the world has fallen in, there are no precedents, wisdom is worthless, and the opinion of one man is as good as that of another,--if not better. So what have you to suggest?

THE GYPSY. Your majesty, before I make my suggestion, let me confess to you that I had underrated the force of your majesty's personality. Not until this moment have I understood that you possess the qualities of kingship as well as the title of king.

THE KING. Well, what of that?

THE GYPSY. This, your majesty. There is only one man in your kingdom who can cope with this girl whom you call mad. Your servants cannot do it. As I passed by the room where she is imprisoned, I heard the soldier whose eye she blacked talking to her. He was saying that it was a great honour to have had a black eye from her hands, and he was begging her autograph. If she had desired to escape, she could have done so--he is her devoted slave. And the doctor who went to examine her as to her sanity has stayed to talk to her about horse-breaking. That, as you know, is his avocation; and he has found in her a woman who knows more about it than he does. He sits there like a man entranced. They are all putty in her hands.

THE KING. (*impatiently*) Get to the point.

THE GYPSY. I have said that there is only one man in the kingdom who can cope with her. And that man is your majesty's self.

THE KING. I?

THE GYPSY. Yes--you must go to her yourself.

THE KING. There's an idea. But what am I to do then?

THE GYPSY. Talk to her, make her your friend. Coax her secret out of her, and you will find that she is some madcap actress from a travelling company of mountebanks, who has done this thing in order to have the story told by the gazetteers and bring people to look at her. Get her to confess, and then let her story spread among the crowd--and the whole uprising that is now taxing the resources of the palace guard will dissolve in a burst of laughter.

THE KING. I will do it. If it is not a kingly duty, I shall at least accomplish it in a kingly manner. Thank you, my friend. But what is this?

THE MAID. (*entering*) Your majesty--

THE KING. Speak. What is it?

THE MAID. Two couriers from the King of Basque have arrived on foam-flecked horses, and ask to see you instantly.

THE KING. Let them wait. I have other affairs in hand. Send them here on the stroke of noon. (*To the Gypsy*) Your explanation may be the correct one. But my own opinion is that she is mad. Whatever it is, I shall soon have the truth.

THE GYPSY. May the fortune of kings attend you!

The King goes out. The Gypsy and the maid seat themselves idly on the edge of the dais.

THE MAID. Poor woman! No doubt she went mad with love of the King, until she imagined herself to be his bride. I can understand that! Poor woman!

THE GYPSY. I am almost sorry for him.

THE MAID. Sorry for *him*? You mean, for *her*!

THE GYPSY. The Princess of Basque needs none to be sorry for her. She can take care of herself--as she proved on the eye of the soldier who locked her up.

THE MAID. Then you believe it? That she *is* the Princess of Basque?

THE GYPSY. I know it. Have I not seen her face?

THE MAID. Then why did you not speak up?

THE GYPSY. Who am I, to interfere in the prenuptial courtesies of a royal pair? Besides, it will give her an insight into the character of her future husband.

THE MAID. You are very unjust to the King, to say that. He is not unkind. He only had her locked up because he thought her demented.

THE GYPSY. Precisely. Oh, she is not one to mind a little rough handling. She gives as good as she gets. She will not hold that against him. But that he should think her mad because she came unattended, at an unexpected hour, with flushed cheeks and laughing lips to meet her lover--!

THE MAID. Because she came climbing in at the window like a madwoman!

THE GYPSY. You think as the King does. For you there are no ways but the way to which you are accustomed. That is sanity to you, and all else is madness. You have a map of life which is like your maps of the world--with all the safe known places marked by their familiar names, and outside you have drawn childish pictures of fabulous beasts, and written, "This is a desert." But I tell you I have gone into these deserts, and found good green grass there, and sweet spring water, and delightful fruits. And beyond them I have seen great mountains and stormy seas.... And I shall go back some day, and cross those mountains and those seas, and find what lies beyond.

THE MAID. Yes, it must be interesting to travel.

THE GYPSY. (*brought down to earth*) Forgive me, child. Do you know, you are very like the King. That is just what he would have said.

THE MAID (*pleased*) Is it?

THE GYPSY. Word for word. You are the feminine counterpart of your ruler. What a pity you cannot help him manage his kingdom!

THE MAID. Hush! Here he comes now! And she is with him!

They rise respectfully. The King enters, followed by the Princess of Basque.

THE KING. We can conduct our conversation better in here. (To the others) Leave us.

THE GYPSY. Yes, your majesty.

They go out.

THE KING. Pray be seated, madam.

THE PRINCESS. In your majesty's presence?

THE KING. I will sit down too. We will sit here together. It is unconventional, but--there is no one to see. Please!

He takes her by the hand and conducts her up the dais to the wide seat. He seats himself beside her.

THE PRINCESS. It is very kind of your majesty to give so much of your time to a troublesome girl.

THE KING. I confess that I find it a pleasure to converse with you. It is a relief from the burden of my royal responsibilities.

THE PRINCESS. I did not know that a king had responsibilities. I thought he stood above such things.

THE KING. My responsibilities are many and grave.

THE PRINCESS. Yes. What are they?

THE KING. It would take too long to enumerate them in detail. Suffice it to say that the happiness of a whole people depends on me.

THE PRINCESS. The happiness of a whole people.... That means: merchants--and clerks--and--

THE KING. And bricklayers. Yes, and truck drivers. They look to me for their happiness.

THE PRINCESS. In what does the happiness of a truck driver consist, O King?

THE KING. I am not sure. But I am going to appoint a royal commission to find out for me.

THE PRINCESS. I can tell you now. The happiness of a truck driver consists in drinking beer with his friends at the tavern in the evening, and taking his sweetheart out to see the royal menagerie on Sunday afternoon. And do you know how you can best sub serve that happiness, O King? By letting him alone, to drink his beer, and make love to his sweetheart.

THE KING. You are wrong. You must be wrong. If the happiness of a people were as simple as that, there would be no need of governments and kings to promote it.

THE PRINCESS. Be thankful, O King, that they do not know that--and that they like to have kings and queens, to whom they give, in their generosity, palaces and horses and--and silken chemises from Astrakhan! Why not enjoy the gifts we have, as the truck driver enjoys his beer and his sweetheart? Let us each have our brief flash of happiness in the sun, O King!

THE KING. Your philosophy is the deadly enemy of mine.

THE PRINCESS. And must we be enemies of each other, too?

THE KING. Never, madam. Let us be friends in spite of our opinions.

THE PRINCESS. Your majesty is very gracious.

THE KING. And now that we are friends, I hope you will not keep up the jest any longer. The lady who is to be my wife and queen arrives in a few hours. You can see how necessary it is that the matter be cleared up before she comes. You will not continue to embarrass me?

THE PRINCESS. Now that we are friends, I will tell you the truth. I am *not* she who is to be your wife and queen.

THE KING. Thank you. And in return, I forgive you freely for all the disturbances you have caused to me and my kingdom.

THE PRINCESS. I am sorry.

THE KING. Of course, you did not understand what you were doing. You did not realize how necessary to a kingdom is the tranquillity which comes only from perfect order and regularity. There has not been such a day as this before in the history of my kingdom. And there will never be such a day again. Tomorrow all will be smooth and regular again.

THE PRINCESS. Smooth and regular! Do you mean that you like things always to be the same, with never any change?

THE KING. I happen to like it, yes. But it is not a question of what one likes. It is a question of what is necessary. Even if I did not like order, I would have to submit myself to its routine. That is what it means to be a king.

THE PRINCESS. And is that what it means to be a queen?

THE KING. In this kingdom, yes. In other places, there may be some relaxation of the traditional rule which compels a queen to be in every way a pattern to her subjects. But the queen of my kingdom will always be a model of perfect womanhood.

THE PRINCESS. And what if she did not wish to be?

THE KING. She would learn that her wishes were unimportant.

THE PRINCESS. And if she refused to learn that?

THE KING. (*grimly*) I would teach her.

THE PRINCESS. (*with flashing eyes*) You mean you would make her obey?

THE KING. That is a hard saying. But this kingdom has not been built up with centuries of blood and toil to be torn down at the whim of a foolish girl. I have a duty to perform, and that is to hand on the kingdom to my descendants as it was handed on to me from my great ancestors, Otho and Magnus, Carolus and Gavaine. And by the blood that once flowed in their veins and now flows in mine, I will so do it--and rather than fail, I would break into pieces a woman's body and a wife's heart.

THE PRINCESS. I understand you fully. And may I go now?

THE KING. First you must tell me who you are and how you came to play this mad prank.

THE PRINCESS. Your majesty, I am only a foolish girl. I will not tell you my name, but I came from the kingdom of Basque.

THE KING. Have you ever seen the Princess, by any chance?

THE PRINCESS. I was in the royal caravan.

THE KING. Then you know the Princess!

THE PRINCESS. Not so well as I thought, your majesty. But I had heard so much talk of her coming marriage and of her great happiness, that there was nothing else in my mind. I dreamed of it day and night.

THE KING. Poor child.

THE PRINCESS. You may well say so. I dreamed of it until I lost all sense of reality, and imagined that I was that happy girl who was going to meet her lover.

THE KING. Madness!

THE PRINCESS. It was madness--nothing else. I thought I was to become free--to throw off the restraints that had chafed me for so long at home. I thought I was going to see everything I wished to see, and do everything I wished to do--to follow every impulse, no matter where it led me--to commit every pleasant folly I chose--and be happy.

THE KING. What queer notions!

THE PRINCESS. I had queerer notions than that. I thought I loved a man that I had never seen. I thought he loved me. I pitied myself and him because we were so long apart, and I burned to go to him. So, while the slow-moving caravan was yet far from its destination, I rose secretly in the night, while the others slept, and saddled the fastest horse in the train. I rode under the stars, with only one thought--his arms about me at the journey's end, his lips on mine. So I came to the city. I scaled the walls, and entered the palace at dawn.

THE KING. But tell me--the wall around the palace is seventeen feet high--

THE PRINCESS. True enough.

THE KING. A guard of soldiers continually marches around it--

THE PRINCESS. Very true.

THE KING. And there are spikes on the top. How did you get over?

THE PRINCESS. That is my secret. The rest I have told you. And now let me go.

THE KING. Tell me one thing more--

THE PRINCESS. Nothing more! I must go! I feel that if I stay any longer, something dreadful will happen!

THE KING. (***taking her hand and detaining her***) What do you fear?

THE PRINCESS. I feel like the maiden in the story who was told that if she stayed till the clock struck, she would be changed into the shape of an animal. Something tells me that if I stay here till the clock strikes, we shall both be transformed into beasts. Oh, let me go!

THE KING. No, wait!

The clock strikes noon.

THE PRINCESS. (*staring at the door*) I am lost!

THE GYPSY. (*at the door, announcing*) The couriers of the King of Basque!

The couriers enter. They stare amazed at the girl seated beside the King.

FIRST COURIER. The Princess!

SECOND COURIER. Here!

The King and the Princess look at each other. Then the King speaks.

THE KING. (*challengingly*) Where should the Princess be, but beside her affianced husband?

FIRST COURIER. We came to tell you that she was missing from the caravan.

SECOND COURIER. We feared for her safety.

THE KING. Your fears were needless.

FIRST COURIER. They told us--

THE KING. Never mind what they told you. You have seen. And now leave us.

THE COURIERS. Yes, your majesty.

They go, the Gypsy following.

THE KING. And now, with apologies for the misunderstanding and delay, let me welcome you to my palace and my arms--my princess and my queen!

THE PRINCESS. You will not hold me to it!

THE KING. We cannot escape it.

THE PRINCESS. But I am no fit queen for you. You know what I am like. You do not want me for a wife!

THE KING. It is not the things one wants, but the things that are necessary....

THE PRINCESS. I will never marry you.

THE KING. You shall marry me tomorrow.

THE PRINCESS. I cannot.

THE KING. The preparations are made for the wedding. Two kingdoms hang on the event.

THE PRINCESS. Let them hang!

THE KING. You, the daughter of my father's ancient foe, are to unite two kingdoms in fraternal amity. Do you understand? War and peace are in the balance.

THE PRINCESS. War?

THE KING. Or peace. It rests with you.

THE PRINCESS. I begin to understand. How strange to think of myself as a peace-offering--a gift from one kingdom to another! Is that what it means to be a Princess?

THE KING. That is what it means.

THE PRINCESS. I had rather be a Gypsy, and choose my lover as I wandered the roads!

THE KING. But you are a Princess, and your choosing is between peace and war. Do you choose war?

THE PRINCESS (*fiercely*) For myself, yes. I would gladly lead an army against you. I would destroy with the sword everything that your kingdom stands for. And you--I would kill with pleasure.

THE KING. You might kill *me*, but the things for which my kingdom stands you cannot kill. They are indestructible. They are older than the world, and will last longer.

THE PRINCESS. (*sadly*) Yes--there was order before the world began its tumult, and there will be quiet when the final night sets in. I am only a spark in the great darkness, a cry in the wide silence.

THE KING. Do you submit?

THE PRINCESS. I am not stronger than death. I submit. I would not have those truck drivers leaving their sweethearts to go to war on account of me. (***She goes up to the curtain, and touches it***.) How thin the prison-wall is! And yet it shuts me away from the sunlight.

THE KING (*gently*) I am a good king, and I shall be a good husband.

THE PRINCESS. It will be easy for you, perhaps. To me it will not come so easy to be a good wife.

THE KING. Put yourself in my hands, and I will teach you.

THE PRINCESS. I will try. (*She kneels at his feet*.) O King, I will be obedient to you in all things. I will obey your commands, and be as you wish me to be--a good wife and a good queen.

THE KING. (*taking her hand and raising her to his side*) For my sake!

THE PRINCESS. For the sake of the truck driver and his sweetheart.

THE KING. As you will.

THE PRINCESS. I ask one small wish--that you leave me now. I must think over my new condition and all that it means.

THE KING. I am happy to see you in so profitable a frame of mind. Let me remind you that the royal luncheon will be served promptly in half an hour.

THE PRINCESS. I shall be there--on time.

THE KING. Meanwhile I leave you to your thoughts.

He goes.

THE PRINCESS. How weak I am! (She goes to the wide seat, and sits down, brooding. The Gypsy steals in, and crouches on the dais beside the wide seat.) A good queen, and a good wife--?

THE GYPSY. (*softly*) Impossible.

THE PRINCESS (*startled*) Was it I said that?

*   *   *   *   *

Night. The curtains are drawn aside. The walls and pillars are silhouetted against a moonlit sky.... The Gypsy is standing by the window, looking out.

THE GYPSY. Ah, nameless and immortal goddess, whose home is in the moonbeams! I speak to you and praise you for perhaps the last time. O august and whimsical goddess, I am about to die for your sake--I, the last of your worshippers! When I have perished on your altar, the whole world will be sane. Your butterflies will no longer whirl on crimson wings within the minds of men; only the maggots of reason will crawl and fester. You will look, and weep a foolish tear--for all this is not worth your grief--and take your flight to other constellations.

THE MAID. (*who has just entered and stands listening*) The constellations! Oh, do teach me astronomy!

THE GYPSY. Astronomy! Why do you want to be taught astronomy?

THE MAID. Because I want to be able to tell fortunes from the stars.

THE GYPSY. That is astrology, my dear--a much more useful science. Come, and I will give you a lesson. Do you see that dim planet swinging low on the horizon? That is my star. Its name is Saturn. It is the star of mischief and rebellion. I was born under that star, and I shall always hate order as Saturn hated his great enemy Jupiter.

THE MAID. One does not need to know the stars to tell that. But let me counsel you to caution.

THE GYPSY. Ah, my dear, that was a wifely speech! You will make a success of marriage.

THE MAID. I shall never marry.

THE GYPSY. It would be a pity not to make some good man happy. You are the ideal of every male being in this kingdom, including its ruler.

THE MAID. Do you really think I am the sort of girl to make the King happy?

THE GYPSY. I am sure of it. You are the very one. You have all the domestic virtues. You are quiet, dignified, obedient. If you have any thoughts or impulses which do not fit into the frame of wifely domesticity, you know how to suppress them.

THE MAID. You are making fun of me.

THE GYPSY. I am speaking the truth. You would make the King a perfect wife. Ah, if only you were the Princess of Basque, and she a child of the gypsies!--Shall I read your fortune from the stars?

THE MAID. Yes!

THE GYPSY. What is your birthday?

THE MAID. I do not know.

THE GYPSY. It is strange for a child of the gypsies not to know that. But I can guess. You were born under the sign of Libra.

THE MAID. How can you tell that?

THE GYPSY. You counselled me to caution. Only one born under the sign of the scales could have made that speech. You have the balanced temperament.

THE MAID. Which is my star?

THE GYPSY. You are sixteen years old. When you were born, the planet housed in the sign of Libra was Venus. And so you will love not too much, nor too little, but well. A fortunate planet! There it is, high in the heavens. And see, it is in conjunction with Jupiter. Do you know what that means?

THE MAID. No! Tell me!

THE GYPSY. It means that love and authority will presently come together in your life.... Oh, happy, happy child!

THE MAID. But I do not understand.

THE GYPSY. There are some things past understanding. Even I do not quite understand it yet. I must think it out.

THE MAID. Then think quickly--and advise me. For I read my fortune otherwise. I see myself growing hollow-eyed with looking in eternal silence at the man I love--and worse than that, at the woman I hate-- for I do hate her. I shall go mad with wanting to speak out my love and hate. Tell me what to do!

THE GYPSY. I cannot advise to rashness. I can only say--speak out your love and hate.

THE MAID. Do you mean--tell him?

THE GYPSY. Yes. Tell him. And do not be afraid. There is no man so proud but he is moved to tenderness when a woman says she loves him. You go to an easy task, my dear, as I go to a hard one. For there is no woman so kind but her heart is stirred with a base triumph and an easy scorn when a man speaks out his love....

They go out. From the other side the King and the Princess come in.

THE KING. I have shown you your apartment. If there is anything wanting to your comfort, name it and it shall be provided.

THE PRINCESS. Nothing is wanting, not even a lock on the door. I shall be happy in my dreams at least.

THE KING. Your delicacy of mind does you credit. I am glad to find that you are not lacking in that supreme attribute of young womanhood-- modesty.

THE PRINCESS. You mistake me. There shall be no lock on the door of my dreams. And I shall meet again in dreams the lover whom I know so well.

THE KING. (*scandalized*) Princess!

THE PRINCESS. Do you put a ban on my dreams, too?

THE KING. I forbid you to discuss such subjects.

THE PRINCESS. Very well. I shall keep my thoughts to myself.

THE KING. Princess, I understand that it is your avocation to be a horse-breaker.

THE PRINCESS. It is one of them.

THE KING. It shall be one of mine to be a woman-breaker.

THE PRINCESS. It is well to know where we stand.

THE KING. You promised this morning to submit yourself to me, and learn to be a good wife.

THE PRINCESS. So I did. And perhaps so will I. I do not know.

THE KING. In what way do I displease you? If it is anything which I can change without hurt to the well-being of my kingdom and the traditions of my ancestors, I will gladly change it.

THE PRINCESS. There are many things--too many to enumerate in detail.

THE KING. Name one of them.

THE PRINCESS. For one thing, you seem a trifle less handsome than the portrait of you they gave me.--But I suppose you have been thinking the same thing about me. Indeed, my portrait must have flattered me greatly, since you did not recognize me this morning....

THE KING. For a moment--it must have been intuition--I did think it was you. Unfortunately, I allowed my judgment to lead me astray.

THE PRINCESS. It always will, if you pay any attention to it. So you did believe it was I for a moment? That is interesting! And how did you feel?

THE KING. I--shall I tell you?

THE PRINCESS. Yes--tell me!

THE KING. I felt embarrassed that I should have been receiving you in my dressing gown.

THE PRINCESS. (*scornfully*) Oh!

She walks away.

THE KING. (*sadly*) I should not have told you about it.

THE PRINCESS. (*coming back to him*) Yes. It was quite right to tell me. And I can see now why you would feel that way. You wanted to look your best for me, didn't you? I quite understand that. I spent weeks trying on my new gowns, and deciding in which one I would seem most beautiful to you. Only, of course, I forgot at the last moment, and rode off to you in this!

THE KING. I--I can understand how you felt. I am--sorry I disappointed you. Forgive me.

THE PRINCESS. Yes. (*After a silence*) I suppose we can be happy together--after a fashion.

THE KING. I am sure of it. And now--shall we go down to the throne-room to rehearse the ceremony for tomorrow?

THE PRINCESS. Please leave me here a while. I want to think.

THE KING. Very well. I shall come for you presently.

He goes.

THE PRINCESS. (*after a pause*) If I make up my mind to it--!

THE GYPSY. (*appearing over the window-ledge*) Never!

THE PRINCESS. Who are you?

THE GYPSY. Say that I am the wind, coming in at your window as I have come so many times before when you lay awake in your chamber, bringing you strange thoughts.

THE PRINCESS. If you are the wind bringing me strange thoughts, you come to me for the last time.

THE GYPSY. Or say that I am a dream that has come to you often in your chamber when you lay asleep.

THE PRINCESS. I am forbidden to dream, now.

THE GYPSY. Or say that I am a Gypsy, come to tell a Queen that he loves her.

THE PRINCESS. Those words are like an echo. I seem to have heard them many times. Come nearer.

He enters, and kneels to her.

THE GYPSY. This is my last folly. I come to you, O princess, and offer all I have--my love, and a bed on the heath under the stars.

THE PRINCESS. That is not enough, my friend. There are other things.

THE GYPSY. What other things?

THE PRINCESS. Dimly, as from another life, I seem to remember the jolting of the wagons that rocked me to sleep, and the good smell of the soup in the big kettle over the fire.

THE GYPSY. (*rising*) This is beyond reason!

THE PRINCESS. All beautiful things are beyond reason, my friend.

THE GYPSY. You are a Gypsy?

THE PRINCESS. I am a Gypsy's sweetheart. Take me away with you.

THE GYPSY. How can we leave this palace?

THE PRINCESS. The way we came.

THE GYPSY. The wall--

THE PRINCESS. Is seventeen feet high. A guard of soldiers continually marches around it. And there are spikes on the top. How did we get over? That is our secret!

THE GYPSY. You have no regrets?

THE PRINCESS. None.

THE GYPSY. Your promise to the King?

THE PRINCESS. I am as mutable as wind.

THE GYPSY. Let us go.

THE PRINCESS. One moment! There is a girl here I am sorry for. Can we not think of some way to help her before we go? She loves the King. Think!

THE GYPSY. I have thought. She is the rightful Princess of Basque-- stolen from her cradle by Gypsies. Tomorrow an old woman from the tribe will come with the proofs. The King will marry her, and they will be happy.

THE PRINCESS. And I am the Gypsy child left in her place! But is it really true?

THE GYPSY. What matters reality to us? *We* are not real.

THE PRINCESS. Good-bye, then, to this place of solid fact that has imprisoned us too long. In another moment we shall melt into the moonlight.

THE GYPSY. Kiss me!

THE PRINCESS. Not here.

THE GYPSY. No. There is a fire in our kisses that would shatter and destroy these comfortable walls. Under the stars, among the winds, we shall quench the hunger and thirst of our love. And there let our dream come true....

THE PRINCESS. Ah, there is a fire in our hearts that will shatter and destroy all comfort, even our own. Not even there, under the stars, among the winds, shall the hunger and thirst of love be quenched. Never shall our dream come true....

THE GYPSY. It is enough that we go to be companions of the winds and stars, wanderers with them....

He leads her to the window.

THE PRINCESS. Over the rim of the world!

They ascend and vanish outside.

POOR HAROLD!

A COMEDY

To DUDLEY FIELD MALONE

This play was first produced in Croton-on-Hudson, N. Y., by the Mt. Airy Players, in 1920, with the following cast:

Harold .... Eugene Boissevain
Isabel .... Doris Stevens
Mrs. Murphy .... B. Marie Gage
Mrs. Falcington .... Crystal Eastman

A room in Washington Square South. By the light of a candle, a young man in tousled hair and dressing gown is writing furiously at a little table. A clock within strikes seven.

A door at the back opens, and a young woman looks in, sleepily. She frowns. The young man looks up guiltily.

SHE. What are you doing?

HE. (*innocently*) Writing.

SHE. So I see. (She comes in, and sits down. It may be remarked that a woman's morning appearance, in dishabille, is a severe test of both looks and character; she passes that test triumphantly. She looks at the young man, and asks)--Poetry?

HE. (*hesitatingly*) No....

SHE. (*continues to look inquiry*).

HE. (*finally*) A letter....

SHE. (*inflexibly*)--To whom?

HE. (*defiantly*) To my wife!

SHE. Oh! That's all right. I thought perhaps you were writing to your father.

HE. (*bitterly*) My father! Why should I write to my father? Isn't it enough that I have broken his heart and brought disgrace upon him in his old age--

SHE. Disgrace? Nonsense! Anybody might be named as a co-respondent in a divorce case.

HE. Not in Evanston, Illinois. Not when you are the local feature of a notorious Chicago scandal. Not when your letters to the lady are published in the newspapers.--Oh, those letters!

SHE. Were they such incriminating letters, Harold?

HAROLD. Incriminating? How can you ask that, Isabel? They were perfectly innocent letters, such as any gentleman poet might write to any lady poetess. How was I to know that a rather plain-featured woman I sat next to at a Poetry Dinner in Chicago was conducting a dozen love-affairs? How was I to know that my expressions of literary regard would look like love-letters to her long-suffering husband? That's the irony of it: I'm perfectly blameless. God knows I couldn't have been anything else, with her. But I've always *been* blameless--in all the seven years of my marriage, I never even kissed another woman. And then to have this happen! Scandal, disgrace, the talk of all Evanston! Disowned by my father, repudiated by my wife, ostracized by my friends, cast forth into outer darkness, and dropped naked and penniless into Greenwich Village!

ISABEL. (*laughing*) Oh, not exactly naked, Harold!

HAROLD. One suit! And that--(*he throws off his dressing gown*) evening clothes! I might as well be naked--I can't go anywhere in the daytime. I tell you I'm not used to this. One week ago I had a house, a motor car, a wife, a position in my father's law-office, a place in society--

ISABEL. That's just it--that's why I was afraid you were writing to your father. He'd send you money, of course. But if you ask him for it, I'll never speak to you again. And as for clothes, you know there's a suit of clothes in there,--a perfectly good suit, too, and I think you're an idiot not to put it on.

HAROLD. Yes. One of Jim's old suits.

ISABEL. Well, what if it is? It would fit you perfectly.

HAROLD. Oh, Isabel! Can't you *see*?

ISABEL. No, I can't see. If Jim is generous enough to give you a suit of clothes--

HAROLD. Yes. That's just it. Jim's girl--Jim's clothes--! Well--
(*sullenly*)--I think Jim's generosity has gone far enough. I'll
be damned if I'll take his clothes.

ISABEL. You're perfectly disgusting. If you weren't a silly poet and
didn't know any better--Yes, Harold Falcington, for a nice boy as you
are in most ways, you have the most antiquated and offensive ideas
about women! *Jim* knows better than to have ever considered me
his property....

HAROLD. (*taken aback by her fierceness*) Good heavens, Isabel, I
didn't mean *that*!

ISABEL. Yes, you did, Harold; but I'm glad you're sorry. It's a good
thing you were thrown out of Evanston, Illinois. It's a good thing you
came to Greenwich Village. And it's a good thing that I've a strong
maternal instinct. If you'll just get the idea out of your head that
you're a ruined man and a lost soul because you've been talked about
and have lost your job in your father's office, and if you'll just stop
thinking that poor dear innocent Greenwich Village is a sink of
iniquity and that I'm a wicked woman--

HAROLD. Isabel! I never said you were a wicked woman! I never thought
such a thing!

ISABEL. But you think you're a wicked man; and so it comes to the same
thing. Look! it's broad daylight. (She goes to the window, and opens
the curtains.) Put out that candle, and read me the letter you've
written to your wife.

She comes back, blows out the candle herself, and sits down

comfortably opposite him.

HAROLD. No, I can't.

ISABEL. Why not? You've read me all the others. Is this just like them? (*Teasingly*)--"Dear Gertrude: I know you will not believe me when I say that I have been the victim of a monstrous injustice, but nevertheless it is true. It has all been a hideous mistake." That's the preamble. Then a regular lawyer's brief, arguing the case--ten pages. Then a wild, passionate appeal for her to forget and forgive. I know how it goes. You've written one every night. This is the seventh.

HAROLD. This one is different.

ISABEL. Good. What does it say?

HAROLD. It says that I am in love with you.

ISABEL. Don't prevaricate, Harold! It says you are now hopelessly in the clutches of a vampire--doesn't it?

HAROLD. (*desperately*) No!

ISABEL. (*warningly*) Harold! The truth!

HAROLD. (*weakening*) Well--

ISABEL. I knew it! That's what you would say. You've told her it's no use to forgive you now.

HAROLD. Yes--I did say that--I don't want her to forgive me, now. I am reconciled to my fate.

ISABEL. Ah--but I'm afraid it's too late, now!

HAROLD. What do you mean?

ISABEL. I mean that your other letters will have done their work. Your wife by this time has been convinced of your innocence--she realizes that she has acted rashly--she is ready to forgive you. And she is probably at this moment on her way to New York to tell you so, and take you back home!

HAROLD. (*frightened*) No!

ISABEL. Yes! If she is not already here and looking for you....

HAROLD. Impossible!

ISABEL. Those letters were very convincing, Harold!

HAROLD. (*shaking his head*) Not in the face of the universal belief of all Evanston in my guilt.

ISABEL. Then she has forgiven you anyway.

HAROLD. (*sadly*) You do not know her.

ISABEL. Don't I? No, Harold, this is to be our last breakfast together. You wouldn't have her walk in on us, would you?--And that reminds me. We're out of coffee. You must go and get some while I dress. And go to the little French bakery for some brioches.

HAROLD. In these clothes?

ISABEL. Or Jim's. Just as you like.

HAROLD. Very well. I shall go as I am. (*Gloomily*) After all, I don't know why I should mind one more farcical touch to my situation. A grown man that doesn't know how to earn his living--

ISABEL. I've suggested several ways.

HAROLD. Yes, acting! No. I'd rather starve.

ISABEL. There are other alternatives.

HAROLD. Yes. Looking over the scientific magazines and finding out about new inventions, and writing little pieces about them and selling that to other magazines!

ISABEL. Why not?

HAROLD. A pretty job for a poet! What do *I* know about machinery?

ISABEL. All the poets I know pay their rent that way. And they none of them know anything about machinery.

HAROLD. All right. I'm in a crazy world. Everything's topsy-turvy. Even the streets have gone insane. They wind and twist until they cross their own tracks. I *know* I'll get lost looking for that French bakery. (*He goes to the door*.) Greenwich Village! My God!

He goes out. She, after a moment, goes into the back room. The charwoman enters, and commences to clean up the place. Isabel comes back, partly clothed and with the rest of her things on her arm, and finishes her toilet in front of the mirror. A sort of conversation ensues.

THE CHARWOMAN. A grand day it's going to be.

ISABEL. (*after a pause*)--Do you think I'm a bad woman, Mrs. Murphy?

MRS. MURPHY. Come, now, it's not a fair question, and me workin' for you. I've no call to be criticizin' the way you do behave. It's my business to be cleanin' up the place, and if 'tis a nest of paganism, sure 'tis not for my own soul to answer for it at the Judgment Day. And a blessed thought it is, too, that they that follow after the lusts of the flesh must go to hell, or else who knows what a poor soul like me would do sometimes, what with seein' the carryin's-on that one does see. But I'd not be breathin' a word against a nice young lady like yourself.

ISABEL. What do you think of Mr. Falcington?

MRS. MURPHY. Well, as my sister that's dead in Ireland used to say, and we two girls together, "Sure," she said, "there's no accountin' for tastes," she said. And you with a fine grand man the like of Mr. Jim, to be takin' up with a lost sheep like this one. But I'd not be sayin' a word against him, for it's a pretty boy he is, to be sure. Well, there's a Last Day comin' for us all, and the sooner the better, the way the young do be shiftin' and changin' as the fancy takes them. I say nothin' at all, nothin' at all--but if you've a quarrel had with Mr. Jim, why don't you make it up with him?

ISABEL. But Jim and I aren't married either, you know.

MRS. MURPHY. It's too soft you are, that's why. You take no for an answer, as a girl shouldn't. Let you keep at him long enough, and he'll give in. Sure the youth of this generation have no regard for their proper rights. Never was a man yet that couldn't be come around, if he was taken in his weakness. A silk dress or a wedding ring or shoes for the baby, it's all the same--they have to be coaxed twice for every one thing they do. It's the nature of the beast, so it is, God help us.

Well I remember how my sister that's dead in Ireland used to say, and we girls together, "Sure," says she, "it's woman's place to ask," says she, "and man's to refuse," says she, "and woman's to ask again," says she. Widow that I am this ten year, I could tell you some things now-- but I'll not be sayin' a word.

ISABEL. Do I look all right?

MRS. MURPHY. It's pretty as a flower you look, Miss. And I'd not be askin' questions, for it's none of my business at all, but who are you fixin' yourself up for to-day, if you know yourself?

ISABEL. What difference does it make? I go into rehearsal next week, and there's a manager that will want to make love to me, and he's fat, and I'll get to hate and loathe the sight of male mankind--and this is my last week to enjoy myself! (*She goes to the door at the back*.) Besides, Jim may have another girl by this time, or Mr. Falcington's wife may come.

She goes into the inner room.

MRS. MURPHY. His wife--God help us!

She shakes her head, and starts to go out.

There is a knock. She opens the door, and admits a woman in a travelling suit.

THE WOMAN. Is Mr. Falcington here?

MRS. MURPHY. (*disingenuously*) There's a party of that name on the east side of the Square if I'm not mistaken, ma'am, in the Benedick, bachelor apartments like--'tis there you might inquire.

THE WOMAN. There's no Mr. Falcington here?

MRS. MURPHY. On another floor, maybe. 'Tis a lady lives here.

The woman turns to go.

ISABEL. (*within*) Who is asking for Mr. Falcington?

THE WOMAN. I am Mrs. Falcington,--his wife.

ISABEL. (*at the inner door*) Oh!

MRS. FALCINGTON. And you are Isabel Summers?

ISABEL. Yes.

MRS. MURPHY. The Lord have mercy!

She escapes.

ISABEL. Sit down.

MRS. FALCINGTON. Thank you. I will. (*She does so.*) Harold is out?

ISABEL. Yes. (*A pause*) Getting brioches for breakfast. (*A pause*) You look tired. Won't you have some coffee? It's ready.

MRS. FALCINGTON. Thank you. Yes.

Both the women give an impression of timid courage.

ISABEL. (*pouring the coffee*) He ought to be back soon. He talked of getting lost in the crooked streets of the Village, and I'm afraid that's what has happened to him.

MRS. FALCINGTON. Yes. Harold is all at sea in a strange place.

She takes the coffee and sips it.

ISABEL. Tell me--how did you know?

MRS. FALCINGTON. (*smiling*) Private detectives.

ISABEL. (*a little shocked*) Oh!

MRS. FALCINGTON. Please don't misunderstand me. I'm not going to make any trouble.... But I did want to know what became of him.

ISABEL. Yes ... naturally.

MRS. FALCINGTON. And then--you see, I wanted to know what you were like; and--and whether he was happy with you. I don't think detectives are very intelligent. They couldn't get it into their heads that I wanted the truth. They gave me a--a very lurid account of--of you. And of course Harold's letters gave me no help. So I came down to see for myself.

ISABEL. (*rising*) Mrs. Falcington: here is a letter that Harold was writing this morning. It tells about me--and I fancy you won't find it so essentially different from the detectives' account. Read it and see.

MRS. FALCINGTON. (*reading the letter*) He says he loves you.

ISABEL. In those words?

MRS. FALCINGTON. No--he says he is involved in a strange and sudden infatuation. But it means the same thing.

ISABEL. No it doesn't. He isn't in love with me. I'll tell you straight--he's in love with *you*.

MRS. FALCINGTON. How do you know?

ISABEL. From the letters he wrote you.

MRS. FALCINGTON. Oh! he showed them to you, did he? How like him!

ISABEL. But he *is* in love with you. And he *isn't* happy with me.

MRS. FALCINGTON. Why not?

ISABEL. He hates this kind of life. He wants order, regularity, stability, comfort, ease, the respect of the community----

MRS. FALCINGTON. He used to tell me all those things bored him to death.

ISABEL. (*pleading*) You *must* take him back!

MRS. FALCINGTON. Don't you want him?

ISABEL. Well--(*she laughs in embarrassment*)--Not that bad!

MRS. FALCINGTON. His father will make him an allowance to live on.

ISABEL. I've told him I would never speak to him again if he took it.

MRS. FALCINGTON. You don't expect him to *work*, do you?

ISABEL. Yes--if he has anything to do with me.

MRS. FALCINGTON. Then if you can make him do that, by all means take charge of his destinies!

ISABEL. But--but--that's not the point. He loves you. He wants to go back. He didn't do any of those things he was accused of, you know.

MRS. FALCINGTON. Did he tell you that?

ISABEL. Yes.

MRS. FALCINGTON. Well--he told a story. (*Isabel is shocked*.) Oh, there's no doubt about it. (*Her tone leaves none*.)

ISABEL. But she was ugly!

MRS. FALCINGTON. Did he tell you that?

ISABEL. Yes! Wasn't she?

MRS. FALCINGTON. There *are* handsome poetesses--a few--and this was one of them. She is one of the most beautiful women in Chicago.

ISABEL. Then he lied....

MRS. FALCINGTON. Oh, yes--of course. He just can't help it. Any more than he can help making love----

ISABEL. You mean this is not the first----

MRS. FALCINGTON. In the seven years of our marriage, he has made love to every pretty woman he came across.

ISABEL. (*sharply*) Why did you stand for it?

MRS. FALCINGTON. Because I was a fool. And because he is a child.

ISABEL. (*almost pleadingly*) He **can** write poetry, can't he?

MRS. FALCINGTON. Yes. Yes! Oh, yes!

ISABEL. Then--I suppose--it's all right. But I'm angry at myself, just the same, for being taken in.

MRS. FALCINGTON. It's strange.... You feel humiliated at having been made a fool of for seven days. I've been made a fool of for seven years, and I've never realized that I had a right to feel ashamed.

ISABEL. That's the difference between Greenwich Village and Evanston, Illinois.

MRS. FALCINGTON. Yes. But when I go back I shall lose the sense of it. I'll think I'm an injured woman because he was unfaithful to me, or because he brought scandal upon the family, or something like that. Now I realize that it's none of those things. It's--it's just an offence against--my human dignity. I've been treated like--like an inferior. But why shouldn't I be treated like an inferior? I **am** an inferior. When I go back to Evanston, and take up grass-widowhood and the burden of living down the family scandal, and sit and twiddle my thumbs in a big house, and have my maiden aunt come to live with me----

ISABEL. But why should you do that? If that's what it means to go back to Evanston, don't go! Stay here!

MRS. FALCINGTON. But--what could I do?

ISABEL. Do? Why--why--go on the stage!

MRS. FALCINGTON. (*rising*) Are you in earnest?

ISABEL. Look here. You've a good voice, and you're intelligent. That's enough to start with. I don't know whether you can act or not--but you'll find out. And if you can't act, you'll do something else. Your people will stake you?--give you an allowance, I mean?

MRS. FALCINGTON. To go on the stage with? Never. But I've a small income of my own. Only about a hundred a month. Would that do?

ISABEL. Do? Yes, that will do very well! And now it's my turn to ask you--are *you* in earnest? Because I am.

MRS. FALCINGTON. You are the first human being who even suggested to me
that I could do anything. I've wanted to do something, but I couldn't even think of it as possible. It *wasn't* possible in Evanston. And as for *acting*, I kept that dream fast locked at the very bottom of my heart, for fear if I brought it out it would be shattered by polite laughter--

ISABEL. You'll have to expose that dream to worse things than polite laughter, my dear.

MRS. FALCINGTON. I can, now. It won't get hurt. I'm free now to take care of my dream--to fight for it--to mike it come true. You have set me free.--I'm going to go and get a room-- *now*!

ISABEL. Let me go with you and help you find one!

MRS. FALCINGTON. And to-morrow--

ISABEL. To-morrow--

Harold enters. He stops short in the doorway, and drops the brioches.
He looks at one woman, then at the other. Suddenly he goes between them
with arms outspread as though to keep the peace.

HAROLD. No! no! I am not worthy of either of you! (They stare at him,
bewildered. He goes on)--Why should you struggle over me? Do not hate
each other! For my sake, be friends! Ah, God, that this tragic meeting
should have happened! And now I must decide between you.... (He goes
to Mrs. Falcington and throws himself on his knees before her.)
Forgive and forget! Come back with me to Evanston!

MRS. FALCINGTON (*over his head to Isabel*) The perfect egotist!

The curtain falls, and then rises again for a moment. Harold is now
on his knees to Isabel.

HAROLD. Marry me!

ISABEL. Harold! You have not been all this time getting brioches. I
smell--heliotrope!

The curtain rises and falls several times, showing Harold on his
knees alternately to the two women, who look at each other above his
head, paying no attention to him.

The Codes Of Hammurabi And Moses
W. W. Davies

QTY

The discovery of the Hammurabi Code is one of the greatest achievements of archaeology, and is of paramount interest, not only to the student of the Bible, but also to all those interested in ancient history...

Religion   **ISBN: *1-59462-338-4***   **Pages:132**

MSRP $12.95

The Theory of Moral Sentiments
Adam Smith

QTY

This work from 1749. contains original theories of conscience amd moral judgment and it is the foundation for systemof morals.

Philosophy   ISBN: *1-59462-777-0*   **Pages:536**

MSRP $19.95

Jessica's First Prayer
Hesba Stretton

QTY

In a screened and secluded corner of one of the many railway-bridges which span the streets of London there could be seen a few years ago, from five o'clock every morning until half past eight, a tidily set-out coffee-stall, consisting of a trestle and board, upon which stood two large tin cans, with a small fire of charcoal burning under each so as to keep the coffee boiling during the early hours of the morning when the work-people were thronging into the city on their way to their daily toil...

Pages:84

Childrens   ISBN: *1-59462-373-2*   *MSRP $9.95*

My Life and Work
Henry Ford

QTY

Henry Ford revolutionized the world with his implementation of mass production for the Model T automobile. Gain valuable business insight into his life and work with his own auto-biography... "We have only started on our development of our country we have not as yet, with all our talk of wonderful progress, done more than scratch the surface. The progress has been wonderful enough but..."

Pages:300

Biographies/   ISBN: *1-59462-198-5*   *MSRP $21.95*

The Art of Cross-Examination
Francis Wellman

QTY

I presume it is the experience of every author, after his first book is published upon an important subject, to be almost overwhelmed with a wealth of ideas and illustrations which could readily have been included in his book, and which to his own mind, at least, seem to make a second edition inevitable. Such certainly was the case with me; and when the first edition had reached its sixth impression in five months, I rejoiced to learn that it seemed to my publishers that the book had met with a sufficiently favorable reception to justify a second and considerably enlarged edition. ..

Pages:412

Reference   ISBN: *1-59462-647-2*

MSRP $19.95

On the Duty of Civil Disobedience
Henry David Thoreau

QTY

Thoreau wrote his famous essay, On the Duty of Civil Disobedience, as a protest against an unjust but popular war and the immoral but popular institution of slave-owning. He did more than write—he declined to pay his taxes, and was hauled off to gaol in consequence. Who can say how much this refusal of his hastened the end of the war and of slavery ?

Law   ISBN: *1-59462-747-9*

Pages:48

MSRP $7.45

Dream Psychology Psychoanalysis for Beginners
Sigmund Freud

QTY

Sigmund Freud, born Sigismund Schlomo Freud (May 6, 1856 - September 23, 1939), was a Jewish-Austrian neurologist and psychiatrist who co-founded the psychoanalytic school of psychology. Freud is best known for his theories of the unconscious mind, especially involving the mechanism of repression; his redefinition of sexual desire as mobile and directed towards a wide variety of objects; and his therapeutic techniques, especially his understanding of transference in the therapeutic relationship and the presumed value of dreams as sources of insight into unconscious desires.

Pages:196

Psychology   ISBN: *1-59462-905-6*

MSRP $15.45

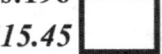

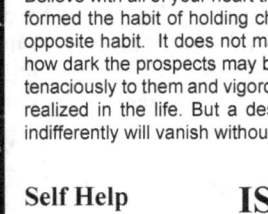

The Miracle of Right Thought
Orison Swett Marden

QTY

Believe with all of your heart that you will do what you were made to do. When the mind has once formed the habit of holding cheerful, happy, prosperous pictures, it will not be easy to form the opposite habit. It does not matter how improbable or how far away this realization may see, or how dark the prospects may be, if we visualize them as best we can, as vividly as possible, hold tenaciously to them and vigorously struggle to attain them, they will gradually become actualized, realized in the life. But a desire, a longing without endeavor, a yearning abandoned or held indifferently will vanish without realization.

Pages:360

Self Help   ISBN: *1-59462-644-8*

MSRP $25.45

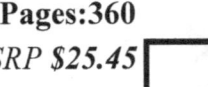

QTY

☐ **The Rosicrucian Cosmo-Conception Mystic Christianity** by *Max Heindel* ISBN: *1-59462-188-8* **$38.95**
The Rosicrucian Cosmo-conception is not dogmatic, neither does it appeal to any other authority than the reason of the student. It is: not controversial, but is: sent forth in the, hope that it may help to clear... New Age/Religion Pages 646

☐ **Abandonment To Divine Providence** by *Jean-Pierre de Caussade* ISBN: *1-59462-228-0* **$25.95**
"The Rev. Jean Pierre de Caussade was one of the most remarkable spiritual writers of the Society of Jesus in France in the 18th Century. His death took place at Toulouse in 1751. His works have gone through many editions and have been republished... Inspirational/Religion Pages 400

☐ **Mental Chemistry** by *Charles Haanel* ISBN: *1-59462-192-6* **$23.95**
Mental Chemistry allows the change of material conditions by combining and appropriately utilizing the power of the mind. Much like applied chemistry creates something new and unique out of careful combinations of chemicals the mastery of mental chemistry... New Age Pages 354

☐ **The Letters of Robert Browning and Elizabeth Barret Barrett 1845-1846 vol II** ISBN: *1-59462-193-4* **$35.95**
by *Robert Browning* and *Elizabeth Barrett* Biographies Pages 596

☐ **Gleanings In Genesis (volume I)** by *Arthur W. Pink* ISBN: *1-59462-130-6* **$27.45**
Appropriately has Genesis been termed "the seed plot of the Bible" for in it we have, in germ form, almost all of the great doctrines which are afterwards fully developed in the books of Scripture which follow.... Religion/Inspirational Pages 420

☐ **The Master Key** by *L. W. de Laurence* ISBN: *1-59462-001-6* **$30.95**
In no branch of human knowledge has there been a more lively increase of the spirit of research during the past few years than in the study of Psychology, Concentration and Mental Discipline. The requests for authentic lessons in Thought Control, Mental Discipline and... New Age/Business Pages 422

☐ **The Lesser Key Of Solomon Goetia** by *L. W. de Laurence* ISBN: *1-59462-092-X* **$9.95**
This translation of the first book of the "Lernegton" which is now for the first time made accessible to students of Talismanic Magic was done, after careful collation and edition, from numerous Ancient Manuscripts in Hebrew, Latin, and French... New Age/Occult Pages 92

☐ **Rubaiyat Of Omar Khayyam** by *Edward Fitzgerald* ISBN:*1-59462-332-5* **$13.95**
Edward Fitzgerald, whom the world has already learned, in spite of his own efforts to remain within the shadow of anonymity, to look upon as one of the rarest poets of the century, was born at Bredfield, in Suffolk, on the 31st of March, 1809. He was the third son of John Purcell... Music Pages 172

☐ **Ancient Law** by *Henry Maine* ISBN: *1-59462-128-4* **$29.95**
The chief object of the following pages is to indicate some of the earliest ideas of mankind, as they are reflected in Ancient Law, and to point out the relation of those ideas to modern thought. Religion/History Pages 452

☐ **Far-Away Stories** by *William J. Locke* ISBN: *1-59462-129-2* **$19.45**
"Good wine needs no bush, but a collection of mixed vintages does. And this book is just such a collection. Some of the stories I do not want to remain buried for ever in the museum files of dead magazine-numbers an author's not unpardonable vanity..." Fiction Pages 272

☐ **Life of David Crockett** by *David Crockett* ISBN: *1-59462-250-7* **$27.45**
"Colonel David Crockett was one of the most remarkable men of the times in which he lived. Born in humble life, but gifted with a strong will, an indomitable courage, and unremitting perseverance... Biographies/New Age Pages 424

☐ **Lip-Reading** by *Edward Nitchie* ISBN: *1-59462-206-X* **$25.95**
Edward B. Nitchie, founder of the New York School for the Hard of Hearing, now the Nitchie School of Lip-Reading, Inc, wrote "LIP-READING Principles and Practice". The development and perfecting of this meritorious work on lip-reading was an undertaking... How-to Pages 400

☐ **A Handbook of Suggestive Therapeutics, Applied Hypnotism, Psychic Science** ISBN: *1-59462-214-0* **$24.95**
by *Henry Munro* Health/New Age/Health/Self-help Pages 376

☐ **A Doll's House: and Two Other Plays** by *Henrik Ibsen* ISBN: *1-59462-112-8* **$19.95**
Henrik Ibsen created this classic when in revolutionary 1848 Rome. Introducing some striking concepts in playwriting for the realist genre, this play has been studied the world over. Fiction/Classics/Plays 308

☐ **The Light of Asia** by *sir Edwin Arnold* ISBN: *1-59462-204-3* **$13.95**
In this poetic masterpiece, Edwin Arnold describes the life and teachings of Buddha. The man who was to become known as Buddha to the world was born as Prince Gautama of India but he rejected the worldly riches and abandoned the reigns of power when... Religion/History/Biographies Pages 170

☐ **The Complete Works of Guy de Maupassant** by *Guy de Maupassant* ISBN: *1-59462-157-8* **$16.95**
"For days and days, nights and nights, I had dreamed of that first kiss which was to consecrate our engagement, and I knew not on what spot I should put my lips..." Fiction/Classics Pages 240

☐ **The Art of Cross-Examination** by *Francis L. Wellman* ISBN: *1-59462-309-0* **$26.95**
Written by a renowned trial lawyer, Wellman imparts his experience and uses case studies to explain how to use psychology to extract desired information through questioning. How-to/Science/Reference Pages 408

☐ **Answered or Unanswered?** by *Louisa Vaughan* ISBN: *1-59462-248-5* **$10.95**
Miracles of Faith in China Religion Pages 112

☐ **The Edinburgh Lectures on Mental Science (1909)** by *Thomas* ISBN: *1-59462-008-3* **$11.95**
This book contains the substance of a course of lectures recently given by the writer in the Queen Street Hail, Edinburgh. Its purpose is to indicate the Natural Principles governing the relation between Mental Action and Material Conditions... New Age/Psychology Pages 148

☐ **Ayesha** by *H. Rider Haggard* ISBN: *1-59462-301-5* **$24.95**
Verily and indeed it is the unexpected that happens! Probably if there was one person upon the earth from whom the Editor of this, and of a certain previous history, did not expect to hear again... Classics Pages 380

☐ **Ayala's Angel** by *Anthony Trollope* ISBN: *1-59462-352-X* **$29.95**
The two girls were both pretty, but Lucy who was twenty-one who supposed to be simple and comparatively unattractive, whereas Ayala was credited, as her Bombwhat romantic name might show, with poetic charm and a taste for romance. Ayala when her father died was nineteen... Fiction Pages 484

☐ **The American Commonwealth** by *James Bryce* ISBN: *1-59462-286-8* **$34.45**
An interpretation of American democratic political theory. It examines political mechanics and society from the perspective of Scotsman James Bryce Politics Pages 572

☐ **Stories of the Pilgrims** by *Margaret P. Pumphrey* ISBN: *1-59462-116-0* **$17.95**
This book explores pilgrims religious oppression in England as well as their escape to Holland and eventual crossing to America on the Mayflower, and their early days in New England... History Pages 268

QTY

The Fasting Cure *by Sinclair Upton*   ISBN: *1-59462-222-1*   **$13.95**
In the Cosmopolitan Magazine for May, 1910, and in the Contemporary Review (London) for April, 1910, I published an article dealing with my experi-
ences in fasting. I have written a great many magazine articles, but never one which attracted so much attention... New Age/Self Help/Health Pages 164

Hebrew Astrology *by Sepharial*   ISBN: *1-59462-308-2*   **$13.45**
In these days of advanced thinking it is a matter of common observation that we have left many of the old landmarks behind and that we are now pressing
forward to greater heights and to a wider horizon than that which represented the mind-content of our progenitors...   *Astrology Pages 144*

Thought Vibration or The Law of Attraction in the Thought World   ISBN: *1-59462-127-6*   **$12.95**

by William Walker Atkinson   *Psychology/Religion Pages 144*

Optimism *by Helen Keller*   ISBN: *1-59462-108-X*   **$15.95**
Helen Keller was blind, deaf, and mute since 19 months old, yet famously learned how to overcome these handicaps, communicate with the world, and
spread her lectures promoting optimism. An inspiring read for everyone...   *Biographies/Inspirational Pages 84*

Sara Crewe *by Frances Burnett*   ISBN: *1-59462-360-0*   **$9.45**
In the first place, Miss Minchin lived in London. Her home was a large, dull, tall one, in a large, dull square, where all the houses were alike, and all the
sparrows were alike, and where all the door-knockers made the same heavy sound.   *Childrens/Classic Pages 88*

The Autobiography of Benjamin Franklin *by Benjamin Franklin*   ISBN: *1-59462-135-7*   **$24.95**
The Autobiography of Benjamin Franklin has probably been more extensively read than any other American historical work, and no other book of its kind
has had such ups and downs of fortune. Franklin lived for many years in England, where he was agent...   *Biographies/History Pages 332*

Name	
Email	
Telephone	
Address	
City, State ZIP	

☐ **Credit Card**   ☐ **Check / Money Order**

Credit Card Number	
Expiration Date	
Signature	

Please Mail to: *Book Jungle*
PO Box 2226
Champaign, IL 61825
or Fax to: *630-214-0564*

ORDERING INFORMATION

web: *www.bookjungle.com*
email: *sales@bookjungle.com*
fax: *630-214-0564*
mail: *Book Jungle PO Box 2226 Champaign, IL 61825*
or PayPal *to sales@bookjungle.com*

Please contact us for bulk discounts

DIRECT-ORDER TERMS

**20% Discount if You Order
Two or More Books**
Free Domestic Shipping!
Accepted: Master Card, Visa,
Discover, American Express